ON A RAZOR'S EDGE

Darkness, 3

by K.F. Breene

Website: http://kfbreene.com/
Blog: www.KFBreene.org
Facebook: KFBreene
Facebook Like Page:
https://www.facebook.com/AuthorKF
Twitter: @KFBreene

Other Titles by K.F. Breene

Skyline Series (Contemporary Romance)
Building Trouble, Book 1
Uneven Foundation, Book 2
Solid Ground, Book 3

Jessica Brodie Diaries (Contemporary Romance)
Back in the Saddle, Book 1 – FREE
Hanging On, Book 2
A Wild Ride, Book 3

Growing Pains (Contemporary Romance)
Lost and Found, Book 1 - FREE
Overcoming Fear, Book 2
Butterflies in Honey, Book 3

Darkness Novella Series (Paranormal Romance)

Into the Darkness, 1 - FREE
Braving the Elements, 2
On a Razor's Edge, 3
Demons, 4
The Council, 5
Shadow Watcher, 6
Jonas, 7
Charles, 8

Warrior Chronicles (Light Fantasy)
Chosen, Book 1
Hunted, Book 2
Shadow Lands, Book 3

On a Razor's Edge

Chapter 1

Andris stalked into the white mage's chamber in a cloud of irritation, ignoring the newest statue, gleaming and gaudy, decorating the far corner of the enormous room. Why anyone needed this much space, he couldn't say, but the room screamed conceit. A large self-portrait hung above a sweeping fireplace, drawing the eye. Mirrors dotted the walls, positioned for the best effect to catch and throw back a glimpse of their master. Bronze sculptures or statues, intent on duplicating the white mage's attributes in some way, littered the tabletops and desk. Unlike Andris's living quarters, which boasted its owner's refined grace and subtle workings, Trek liked flashy and extravagant.

"White Mage," Andris said with a slight bow. Trek demanded formalities: bowing, titles, and often whimpering from those who reported to him.

Those that reported to him…

That concept was beginning to rankle. Trek was blind to his surroundings, unorganized, and completely unable to lead. Andris had not only found him, trained him, and shown him the underbelly of magic working, but he'd *put* the sniveling fool into his position. At first Andris had gone along with Trek's illusions of grandeur in order to manipulate him more easily. Now, however, he saw his error. The younger man was starting to don his position like a lead suit in the ocean—he bullied others and created dissension within the ranks. Basically, instead of working together to create a team of power, as a mage and leader should, he was dismembering their advantages.

Andris took a deep breath. He couldn't set that issue straight at the moment. He had more important loose ends to knot together.

"Ah, Andris, yes." Trek walked at a measured pace to a large, throne-like chair. His pretentious white cape billowed behind him as he sat. "Have you been able to solve the mystery of how those skulking rejects were able to find our secret fortress? My enchantment, not to mention the underground facility, should have prevented that."

"I believe Stefan is linked in some way to the girl. He is often able to pinpoint her whereabouts when no one else can."

"I see. I thought it was something like that. Fine. Any ideas as to how she was able to suck all my power out? I could have burned Stefan from the face of the earth had that strike landed."

"My source in his establishment did not know. They say her magic does not operate like ours, but they don't know any more than that. Their Regional and his linked mage are expected within the week to assess."

"Yes, your *source*. The same source that gave the task to capture the girl to an incompetent *boy.*"

Andris curled his hand into a fist. "He did actually deliver the girl. Unfortunately, we didn't have the information we needed when she was in our possession."

"True. The black power level has always been a myth. Hmm. How do you plan to amend your failures, then?" Trek's magic crackled with the implied threat.

Andris barely suppressed his chuckle. Maintaining an even voice, he said, "My source wasn't able to get close to the girl without being detected, but with the Regional coming, there is room to amend that. The girl is untrained. We need to make the grab soon, before she learns to work with her power."

Trek nodded slowly, his fingers intertwining on his lap. "I'm sure I don't have to impress upon you how important it is that we get that girl. With her, no one can stand in our way. Not even that group of wrinkly Council members with their circle of white mages. No one! Even if she fails to work with us, which I doubt since you have your ways, I can grow stronger with her blood. I can create *Dulcha* with exceedingly more power. Maybe even demons. She is the key."

The lack of speed at which the idiot came to his conclusions was almost awe-inspiring. "Logic, yes, you have some. Splendid."

The other man's eyes flashed. Definitely a problem for another day.

"I'm already on it," Andris stated smoothly. "I am simply informing you of my…our progress."

"Good then. Carry on." Trek waved him away with a regal posture.

With a slight nod, Andris turned and stalked from the room.

The human was a huge roadblock. She wasn't even trained and she had been able to suck all the magic from the room at that last battle. That form of magic did not translate to Andris's knowledge. If she did learn to use it before they could capture her, she'd be a huge problem to both their way of life, and also their agenda. The enemy would cash in and use her to crush Andris and the other usurpers. All Andris had done thus far would be useless.

She was a great pivot in this war, the winner largely decided by which side she chose. Being that she had allowed Stefan to mark her, clearly she'd already chosen a side, and this left them with two options: use her for her blood, or kill her. Andris would not hesitate to do what was needed. He just had to get close to her.

Which meant he needed to make a call. What good were spies if you never used them?

Chapter 2

A smile flashed across Stefan's breathtakingly handsome face in the failing evening light. "You are so hell bent on not blasting me, you aren't working the blade. Try again."

I bounced from foot to foot like a football player waiting for *hike.* Stefan stood in front of me, large sword held lightly, waiting for me to strike. I feinted left and dove right, slashing with my very sharp dagger. The blade hacked down toward his forearm, making me squint in fear that I would hit him, until he easily shifted at the last second. The blade swept by toward the ground.

Stefan's laughter echoed off the trees as he wrapped his big tattooed arms around my middle to keep me from landing on my head.

This was his special tutoring. Getting up before nightfall, sneaking out to the wooded area behind his mansion, hanging out in a bunch of trees, and laughing at me as he tried to teach me to use my dagger. I failed to see the humor.

"That was good," Stefan commended. "I like the feint. Believable."

I sighed with the feel of him. His strength. His *power.* The man was made well. Very well.

"Hmmm, chocolate chip cookies. I would love to eat you right now." His lips trailed up my neck as tingles worked between my thighs. I melted into his arms as he sucked the hot skin on my neck. "But we need to get you using that dagger, so I'll wait."

"We have plenty of time for training," I breathed.

Ignoring my roaming hands, he propped me up, held me away from him for a moment so my Gumby legs could straighten out, then stepped away with a mouth-watering smile.

I tried to force my frazzled brain back to the situation. "Except, I missed with that feint. Which, don't get me wrong, is a good thing, since if I'd hit you you'd be missing an arm, but still. I can't be *that* good. My comic timing, however, seems to be perfect..."

"Sorry, lovely, I can't help it. Your face goes through all these expressions. Determination first, pa-zazz with the feint, fear when you think you'll get me, and finally relief right before you land on your face. It's comical. You have no poker face."

"You've known how to play poker for, literally, forty-eight hours. How would you know about poker face? And what is a *pa-zazz* face?"

Stefan laughed again. "I've been beating you at poker for, *literally,* the last twenty-four hours," he mocked. "I like that we upped the stakes. The sexual benefits make it much more fun."

Being without much money of my own my whole life, I'd always played poker with friends for tokens. Stefan didn't really get the point of the card game using peanuts, though, so I switched it to strip poker. That got his attention. Then he got the idea to bet sexual favors.

He got really good shortly thereafter. I found myself in some pretty kinky poses with other…paraphernalia that turned out to be quite a lot of fun—for special occasions.

"Beginner's luck," I commented sourly. "And that was only one game."

"Several hands in one game, yes. With lots of breaks for touching. I'm one-for-two. After the end of tonight, I'll be two-for-three. And pleasured often."

"Okay, Texas Hold 'Em, focus for one second. Why can't I make you bleed?" I got back in my ready stance: hands out, knees slightly bent, balls of my feet.

"I'm the best."

"And modest to boot."

He shrugged, waiting patiently for me to try and kill him.

I lunged without warning, jabbing for his heart. He stepped right lazily, flicking my dagger away with his sword, the tattoos on his arms glowing gently.

"You aren't connecting with your magic. That's the problem." He focused on my red blade. "You need to use all your power, not just your safety zone."

"I don't want to blow you up, Stefan," I answered seriously, jogging to a stop three paces beyond him. "Red at least is manageable if something goes wrong. If I use black, who knows, you know?"

His smile dwindled. His black eyes regarded me softly. "We have help coming. They'll know how to train you. They'll know what to do."

What he was too kind to say was, "They'll know why your magic doesn't work like everyone else's." His hope, and mine, was that they could explain why I was different.

All I wanted was to fit in. But Fate continually wanted me the butt of every joke. We were at war, Fate and me. And guess what, Fate was winning. And an asshole.

"Okay, more power, coming up." I breathed deeply, opening to the world around me.

Instantly a gush of power flooded my body, raging and flowing, pushing in to fill up every inch. I sent Stefan a panicked look.

Immediately he was there, through the link between us, using his special ability to smooth it all out. Temper it. Balance it.

Elation tingled as the magic swirled and pooled, stretching my skin, making me high. When he was within me, balancing it all out, *God* I felt good. Masterful. Freaking fantastic!

"Hee yaw, waaka waaka." I bounced like a boxer and shook out my limbs. "Feeling good. Feeling really good."

Stefan nodded slowly, his beautiful onyx eyes twinkling. "It gives the feeling of ecstasy if it's balanced right. The blood link—the tie to me—boosts it tenfold, though. It never felt as good to hold max capacity before we developed the blood link."

His love for me, pulsing through the link, warmed my insides. I smiled like a fool before reality came crashing down. "It seems like it's getting worse, though. I give a soft tug on the elements and I get a flood, whereas before, I had to actively pull before the avalanche came down."

All remnants of a smile vanished. "Starting after puberty, we get stronger the more we work with the elements. It's a steady climb until we reach maximum potential, which happens in everyone at different times. Maybe it's similar with you."

"The more I work with the elements, the more open I am to receive them?" I frowned at him. It kind of made sense. "Except I'm already at full power."

"You've had a rough control over your magic for years without knowing it. You've had more than enough time to reach max potential, but maybe now, being more open with the elements, it'll come easier."

"But why is it such a struggle to contain it all?" I asked sullenly, punctuating the question by stabbing the air.

Stefan minutely shook his head as he studied my mood. "But you do have a lot of power, and with me to balance it out within you, you *are* learning control. With some better instruction, and your intuition, you'll be dynamite."

I couldn't help but chuckle. "Dyn-o-mite."

I got a quirked head in response.

"Never mind. There's no use in us trying to figure this out. Let's just hope the guy that's coming has a clue."

Stefan dropped his sword and stepped forward so fast I got a nervous flutter he was attacking me. Only, I was still too slow to jab him. He flicked away my dagger and laid a palm on my cheek. "He will. We'll figure this out, you and me. You aren't in this alone. I've pledged my life to you—I'm in this with you, whatever it turns out to be."

My eyes misted over with the sentiment. His soft lips brushed mine, the kiss slow and ardent. Expressing his love. Speeding up my heart.

I slid my hand down his defined chest and let it rest on his bumpy abs. "I can't figure out control over my magic, but I can figure out how to poke things, so I guess I'll get good at that until these mysterious helpers roll through."

He gave me one last soft kiss before backing up. His lips curled into a smile. "That's my girl. Learn to kill monsters while you're waiting for the next great thing."

"The next big thing. Is here. That's an ad. I swear, you and Charles are researching my quirks in the wrong ways. My crazy is not a human problem—it's specific to me."

"It's a good place to start. And the next big thing has been here. Or didn't you remember getting pounded by it when you woke up?"

I rolled my eyes. "No need to get crude—you're a man, I hear you roar. Now, prepare to die."

I lunged at him, magic racing through my limbs, buzzing through my midsection. He rolled away from my blade, barely missed. His glowing sword came up as my dagger sped toward his midsection, blocking at the last moment. On the move again.

"As—□ He feinted, making me pivot at the last second, falling behind.

"You—□ His sword rushed toward me, causing me to take two fast steps left and smash my dagger against his steel. He was already moving again.

"Wish!" The very tip of his blade flicked at my ribcage, opening a little tear in my shirt.

I flinched back, panting. Hands on knees, I caught my breath while huffing out a laugh. "Charles had you watch some of the romantic comedies, huh?"

"A few."

"Had a good laugh at the men in them, I'd bet."

"Soft men paired with soft women. That fits."

I straightened up, confronted by his lighthearted smile. "And I am…?"

"Irresistible. Beautiful. *Mine*."

Warm fuzzies permeated my chest. Until he finished with, "Also from a race with terrible romance movies."

His laughter echoed once again. I figured it was a great time to try and jab him unexpectedly.

*****

A week later I rolled over as the sun sank from the sky. Stefan and I stayed together every night, often in his private wing within the mansion. He had a giant, spacious bedroom with bathroom, and an outer room with couches, a living room with a gigantic TV, and a weight room.

I'd never lived in so much space in my life. It was good to be king. Or at least sleeping with the leader…

A nervous flutter sped up my heart.

I ran my hand up the smooth skin on his chest, taut with muscles.

"Are you nervous?" I asked, feeling him stir and turn his brawny body toward me.

"Yes, a little. I haven't seen the Regional since he made me the Boss. I'm worried he won't find things up to his exacting standards."

"And he's the leader of…"

"Basically a large, worldwide company. We are broken into smaller satellites. I run this region, one of a hundred in North America. He oversees half of North America—the southern half."

"And someone oversees him?" My hand headed south along his body.

"Yes. And his superior, a she, is overseen by a committee."

My hand closed around his large shaft. His breathing hitched.

"Okay, then why doesn't this Regional guy end the feud between you and the Caped Crusader?"

"There are two factions of my people. The first realize that humans, even though they aren't as large, strong, fast, or able to access their magic easily, have a population far exceeding our own. Not to mention they have more powerful weapons. Imposing ourselves on their societies would only make them afraid. And everyone knows what humans do when acting out of fear. There are still those of us who remember the witch burnings, the Crusades, and the Inquisition. We are a different branch of species of human, basically, but we die just as easily. Well...not just as easily, but we do die."

"And the other faction?"

"The most extreme of them think they should take their place as the dominant species. Most, however, would be happy to just live among humans."

"So, the worst of them want to kill and maim. Like they do now, but without being in the shadows."

"Correct. There's no better way to incite mass violence in humans then to have large, scary creatures try to threaten a human's way of life. Hell, humans don't even suffer their own when it comes to property and position. We stand no chance. Right now we stick to the shadows and we co-exist quietly. We stick our neck out—even to just share openly—and the humans will shoot a hole in it. Trek doesn't seem to understand that, but then, the power-hungry rarely see beyond their delusions of grandeur. Which is why we present them with lots and lots of violence."

"Don't bring a sword to a gunfight."

Stefan's hand massaged up the inside of my leg as my hand picked up speed along his shaft. "Oh, we have guns. We just can't maintain magic with the bullets. Shoot one of Trek's magic creations through the heart, and you get a loud noise and no results."

"I'd always wondered. Huh. But you could shoot each other."

"Yes, we could. And have. But then the cops get called, and that whole sermon about keeping under the humans' radar…"

"I get it, I get it. All right."

His fingers brushed against my sex. "You can be taught." He laughed, his lips pressing against mine.

I spread my legs as his fingers dipped into me, his thumb applying pressure to the sensitive top, making slippery circles. I breathed deeply, my body warming from his ministrations. I'd never felt like I did with Stefan. Even before I'd met him, his body had called to me, begging me to cross whatever distance separated us and wrap myself around him. Though we hadn't uttered the "L-word" to each other yet, we felt it. Both of us did. We felt it like normal people didn't. A deep-rooted connection attached us, not only relaying our emotions through a link between us, but merging our souls into one, then delivering each half to a body.

I climbed onto his large body, eager to feel that rush. The tip of his manhood rubbed along my folds, getting them nice and slick. I leaned up, positioned him, then slowly sat down, accepting him deeply into me. My sex stretched over him, feeling that glorious fullness, pushing all the breath from my lungs.

His palms reached up to me, cupping my breasts, rubbing a thumb along each nipple. I rocked over him, building that wonderful friction, my body winding tight, soaking in the sensations. Tighter and tighter I strove, bobbing on top of him, my head falling back as the tremors gathered and lit me on fire. My body started to sweat, his as well, as his hips thrust up to my downward motion.

"Oh, Sasha," Stefan breathed, eyes closed in determination.

My core vibrated, pulsed, constricted…then blasted apart. A glorified scream filled the room as I exploded in pleasure. I lay my body on top of his, my head resting in the groove of his neck and shoulder as I came down.

"What will happen to us, Stefan?" I asked softly, enjoying the feeling of his fingers trailing along my back.

"We will stay together no matter what comes."

"But what about your mate? You need one, and from what Charles says, she has to have lineage and birthing ability and all sorts of crap that I don't have."

"You might have."

"I'm a human. By default I'm not mate material. Just ask that ginger in my class that hates me."

Stefan tucked a piece of hair behind her ear. "We'll stay together. I'll bring the matter before the Regional and see what he says."

"I can't share you any more than you can share me, Stefan, regardless of your duty."

He kissed my shoulder. "I know, love. I know that. We'll figure it out."

Another half hour had me showered and in combat boots and yoga clothes, striding toward the living room where my bodyguard, Charles, the youngest member of the Watch Command, waited. As usual, the giant muscled guy, dressed in leather from head to foot, sat on the leather couch, knitting some hideously colored monstrosity.

"What are you making this time?" I inquired, snatching an apple out of the fruit bowl resting on the coffee table.

"Well, since you never wear the scarf I made you, I am making a blanket this time."

"Is it for a little girl?"

Charles stopped in his work and surveyed the thee-by-four square foot of fabric. "No, why? What's wrong with it?"

"Charles, it's fluorescent green and pink! Who do you know, who isn't a three-year-old girl, who wants a blanket made with these two colors?"

Charles's bushy eyebrows rumpled on his striking face. "You couldn't have mentioned this *before* I started?"

"Eyes and logic, Charles, they're a lethal combination."

Charles dropped his masterpiece-in-making into his knitting bin beside the couch. He followed me out, headed toward magic class.

"Charles, how am I not considered evil?"

"You're a female. Of *course* you are considered evil."

"Yeah, hilarious. But seriously, if I can wield the black magic level, and Trek does white, doesn't that make me evil?"

"Nah. Magic isn't evil or good. It just *is*. The wielder is the asshole. And the colors are just that. Colors. We've identified their output in power, but the actual color doesn't mean anything."

"And why is black so rare?"

Charles shrugged. "The higher power levels become more rare as they progress. White is super rare. And then black is beyond, I think, so rarer still. It probably wouldn't be as much if humans would admit that magic exists somewhere besides crystal balls and Tarot cards. Instead, they dump their magic into technology and create some truly fantastic things. I'm all for the way things turned out. If humans could procreate like rabbits *and* wield all sorts of magic, we'd be in serious trouble."

"I thought you were working on your ability to summarize."

"Nope. You just continue to hope."

"I do, yes."

We walked into an empty elements class.

"No class today, which you would know if you bothered to read the bulletin." A harried teacher, Andrew, turned to us. "Oh. Well, *you two* will probably be needed with the Boss. Doesn't *anyone* read the bulletins?"

"Don't blame Charles," I said with a dour face. "He can't read at all."

"Oh, you're on fire today. What the hell did I ever do to you?" Charles asked with his hands on his hips as Andrew rolled his eyes and turned away.

"Burnt down my damn apartment, Charles, or don't you remember past yesterday?"

"Get over it. You got a sweet set-up. I did you a favor. And, you nag."

"What does that have to do with the price of apples?"

Charles cocked his head as we shuffled out. "Apples? Who said anything about apples? Did the Boss accidentally take too much blood, or something? You're starting to lose it."

"So, now what?" I asked, happy-go-lucky now that I had a furlough.

"Sure, change the subject. Why have a straightforward, intelligent conversation when we can jump all over the place."

I laughed. "Let me dumb myself down so we can have that conversation."

"I'm not the one that flunks every test she takes."

I nodded, my chest so tight I felt like I might crack a rib. "Touché. Got me there."

Charles smirked, his smile falling back into a grim line of lips a second later. "You're not that clever, you know. I can tell you are nervous as hell. You always turn into a real strange bitch when you're freaking out."

"A real strange bitch." Ice formed in my stomach. "What if it's me? What if I'm the problem, and not the teachers? What if my magic is defunct for some reason?"

Charles shrugged, settling with me on a cold stone bench just outside the mansion. "We'll figure it out. The Boss will tear down the world to keep you safe. And I'm his right-hand man, so between the two of us, we'll make this all work out."

I leaned against his huge body for support. He'd become my best friend. I couldn't imagine getting through all that I had without him, requests for sex and all. "What now?"

"We wait to be called, I guess. And don't get too close. I don't want the Boss tearing my arm off."

I scoffed out a laugh, and stayed where I was.

*****

"They're waiting for you in the purple lounge, Boss."

Stefan nodded to Jameson and imperceptibly took a deep breath. It was always disconcerting when meeting a superior, but this visit would decide his fate. He loved a human. More than that, he was *one* with a human. They shared something indescribable. A love so deep it had turned into something else entirely. Giving her up would be like giving up food. Or sleep. He needed her to survive.

Which was not something he could go around telling his higher-up. His kind didn't mate with humans. They might beget their offspring by that means, since humans could blink and get pregnant, but his species didn't settle down to a life with humans. Not traditionally speaking.

Stefan snorted at himself. He was picking up Sasha's penchant for being cockamamie.

Still, it had to be acknowledged that even though he might break custom and mate a human, he couldn't expect his people to accept her as their leader. He couldn't proclaim her lineage and the right of her station. All she had was her magic, and his devotion.

Devotion. Now that was a word that could get you beat up.

Steeling himself, his face the customary stern mask he wore in public, he entered the purple lounge with a confident step.

Two men waited patiently, elegantly lounging in the large, overstuffed armchairs as if they owned the mansion and the people in it. Stefan's eyes burned into Dominicous, the Regional, with the intensity of an alpha whose territory has been encroached upon. It took one full, vicious beat to rip his gaze away and to the floor, uncomfortably acknowledging his place as lesser.

He didn't remember that ever galling as much.

"You are just barely on the safe side of a challenge," Dominicous stated in elevated speech, albeit colored with humor, which originated from somewhere in Europe a great many decades ago. Stefan's people didn't live forever, but they did live a long damn time.

"But still on the safe side, Regional."

"Quite. Please, sit amongst us. We have much to discuss."

Stefan settled into a chair, his chest turned toward the Regional with the respect due his station, Stefan's eyes able to meet his superiors now that he'd acknowledged the other male's status. Hard brown eyes of brutality in a weather beaten face stared back. You didn't get to be the Boss without being able to hold your own against an entire clan. You didn't become Regional without that same trait, only against a helluva lot more people.

Dominicous extended a scarred hand toward the other man sitting in the room. "This is Toa. He is my linked mage and excels in intricate magical working and application. He is the strongest *white* outside of the Council."

He pronounced it like "toe." Sasha would get a kick out of that if she was privileged enough to meet him.

Long, straight hair so blond it might've been white framed Toa, while cold blue eyes stared out of a pristine face. With such smooth skin and beautifully elegant features, this male appeared feminine. Those eyes, though, sent a chill to the core of Stefan. Death lived in those eyes.

Stefan's hackles rose, another challenge slipping into his gaze before he had to, once again, drag his eyes downward.

"Again, just barely on the safe side of a challenge. It seems you are outgrowing your post," Dominicous remarked lightly.

"No, Regional. Haven't seen a superior in some time."

"I see. On to business, or would you rather a few minutes to discuss pleasantries?"

"Business would do me fine."

"Splendid." The Regional bowed his head, his gaze focused on his scuffed fingernails before he went on. "First order of business. We have had a startling request from this clan. A female with the black power level. Is this correct?"

"Correct. A human."

"Yes."

If that bothered either of them, Stefan would never know. Blondie hadn't moved more than his eyes since Stefan had come into the room.

"And you have marked her, is that correct?" Dominicous continued.

Stefan tried to emulate Blondie but it felt like fire ants danced up his back. "It is."

"We will come back to that." Dominicous draped one long leg over the other, a gesture Stefan recognized as Dominicous' version of comfort. "You know, I assume, that the black power level is so rare it is nearly a myth. It requires a different type of training since the magic reacts differently than what we deem "normal." Sometimes the black level is a disguise for a lower level white. A strange mix of power and use, you see. We've had a few proclamations of the black level this year alone. All were false."

The fire ants started to bite down.

"Toa has come all this way, however, to make sure," Dominicous continued. "We like to be thorough where this is concerned. Finding a black power level would…tip certain battles in our favor. Even if those battles are not officially acknowledged."

Blondie's stare was starting to get irritating.

"So, we shall test her momentarily. There is another subject that needs discussion. Our Council has entered into an agreement with the North American *Mata*—or, to the layman, Shape Changers." Dominicous paused for effect.

Stefan wanted to tell him to get on with it. He knew what the hell they called themselves, and didn't care. They were a nuisance, under the impression that because they *actually* changed into animals, rather than just embodying some of the customary territorial and aggressive traits of animal hunters, like Stefan's species, that their claims to territory should be upheld. They had a magic of sorts, sure—certainly more defined than that of traditional humans—but they couldn't hold a candle to Stefan's clan in the fighting realm. They had tried. And gotten a smack down. Nobody fucked with Stefan's clan, even a white mage. Period.

"We believe the upheaval of those wanting to proclaim themselves to humans—I believe one of their faction reside in this city—the Eastern Territory." At Stefan's nod, Dominicous continued, "They are seeking to unite with other non-human entities. There are a few that could pose a real threat if amassed in numbers. The *Mata* are one."

Stefan didn't like where this was going. And gods be damned, he was about ready to bash Blondie's head against the table to stop that flat-eyed stare.

"We have made an agreement, as I said, with the Alpha of the *Mata*. All those in his influence will unite. It is shaky ground, as I am sure you know. Our kind and theirs don't get along well. And haven't for centuries upon centuries. But we need them, and they will eventually need us when the scientists figure out what the rare strand of cancer that creates the ability to change shape really is. And really does."

"And how does this relate to me directly?" Stefan asked with a calm he didn't feel.

"I think you know."

Stefan couldn't help a flex. "We have a standing truce with them, for now. They don't come in my territories, I don't intrude on theirs."

"That is not enough. You must unite forces. You must be able to fight together. Nolan, the male leading the upheaval against our kind staying in the shadows, has a rare talent for speech. He bends people to his will, promising power, world domination, and other such nonsense. Mages are particularly keen for power, craving it more than most, and flock to his side. We have greater numbers, but he is gathering greater power."

"We fight completely different than the *Mata*. We command, and follow commands, differently."

"We don't anymore, actually. As you will find out, because you will bridge that gap. It is necessary."

Might as well learn to fly while I'm at it.

Stefan barely acceded, causing Dominicous to tilt his head a fraction. It was a thin and dangerous line Stefan walked, but he wasn't having an easy time bowing to another male. Especially since Stefan could take him. It'd be one hell of a fight, but in a dead heat, Stefan could crush him and rip his mantle out from under him.

All in due time. He had to ensure Sasha's safety before he took any steps.

"We will discuss the details tomorrow. Now, let us see to this claim of black power. Bring her in."

Stefan rose easily, relaxing his body as he moved. If Sasha didn't wield black, she could still wield a form of white, which meant she was still mage material. He knew for a fact that her power level exceeded his. He'd felt it both in her blood, and when she used him for an offshoot to sucking all the power from the room. She could download magic like a giant computer could data.

Why the hell was he so worried?

Worried. Another word that would get him beat up.

"Bring her," Stefan barked at Jameson as he poked his head out the door.

When he'd returned to his seat, Dominicous said, "Tell me about the mark. It is a clever business move that might bite you if I take her for my own."

A surge of pure rage shot through Stefan. He stared at the Regional, not bothering to disguise the challenge. He would lose everything, including his life, before he allowed this male to take her like some piece of property. He had wanted to do this delicately, to try to explain matters, but under this sort of pressure, Stefan only knew one course of action. *Kill!*

"I see," Dominicous said quietly. "Not business, then. Interesting. We will return to this challenge at a later date, should it prove necessary. Now, this is her—□

The Regional cut off, his eyes widening in surprise. The unexpected hitch finally dislodged Blondie's constant, flat stare, his attention swiveling toward the entrance.

Sasha stood there, awkwardly, inching closer as though afraid to confront a room full of vipers. She unclasped her hands long enough to give a strange little wave, her face turning bright red. "You called for me?"

Her beautiful eyes met Stefan's and his heart swelled, love and heat filling the blood link they shared as they took comfort in each other's closeness. The world fell away for a moment, one half of a soul meeting the other, before their surroundings again took solid form. It was a strange occurrence that seemed to happen each time they met after any sort of distance.

"Please, come in," Dominicous said, rising.

The door closed behind her, making her jump, before her eyes rose to meet the Regional. Her brows furrowed and her head tilted, meeting his stare not with fear, as one might expect, or even anxiety for her fate, but as though she knew his face and was trying to place him.

"Please," the Regional said as he gestured her forward, his voice an octave higher, rising as though talking to a child.

Vague confusion bled through the link as she took a couple more steps, her curiosity having her glance at the other male in the room.

"Oh, my God!" A grin lit up her face. "He's not…?" She pointed at Blondie and excitedly looked at Dominicous. "He's not a vampire, right? He's one of you guys? One of your kind, or whatever?"

Blondie finally had someone new to stare at.

"What is your name, please?" Dominicous asked in a soft voice. He seemed too damn near demur to her. Stefan expected flat or distant, since she was a human, but this was throwing him for a loop.

"Sasha." She tucked a strand of flyaway hair behind her ear.

"Sasha, I am Dominicous, and this is Toa." Dominicous extended a hand out toward his partnered mage. "He will be testing you. If you have a certain level of power, he will remain in this area and train you. If not, we will decide what's next. Does that sound acceptable?"

Sasha nodded mutely, studying Dominicous's face with squinted eyes, as if she was looking into the sun and remembering a dream at the same time. "Fire away."

Chapter 3

I watched as Toa stood gracefully, moving his body like a ballet dancer. He glided in front of me, almost hovering. If this guy wasn't a real vampire the myths absolutely came from him! Porcelain face almost devoid of all color, smooth and soft, he had pink lips and long black lashes. There was an ethereal look about him. His defined body oozed sensuality, almost feminine in its overtones, and definitely feline. Graceful and lithe, I was totally looking for giant fangs stained with blood.

"Call the elements, please," he requested in a musical voice.

I couldn't get over it! The guy was a vampire. He had to be. Stefan had missed some important details about the magical world, I was sure of it.

Back on track, though still distracted, I drew in all four elements, stopping at red like I usually did.

"Fill up, Sasha," I heard Stefan instruct.

A look at him had me sighing. Having all that power at my disposal freaked me out, especially because it had to go somewhere, and usually ended up in some sort of creative magical experiment that Charles had to then kill.

Trusting Stefan, I opened on up, having to immediately fight the elements as they filled me with magical Prozac, my body starting to sing and dance and crave to draw in more. "How much should I draw?"

Toa stood staring at me, his ice blue eyes reminding me of the middle of a glacier—right before a huge chunk broke off and caused a tidal wave. "All."

"That'll make me pass out." I let in a bit more, stuffing up all available space in my body. Fighting with it. Needing to bend it, or shape it, or run out of here to release it, or this room would need a serious redecoration.

"As much as you can, then."

Toa was irritatingly calm. Plus, did the man ever blink? It was weird.

"It'll make me pass out." *And probably skirt the edges of magic shock.*

"Go until you feel the warning, Sasha," Stefan helped.

I hated doing this. Ever since I had to stop Trek, white mage, from killing people by robbing all his—quite substantial—stockpile of magic, I shied away from overloading. But these guys were here for a reason, and this was important to Stefan, so I drew in more until I felt the prickles on my skin.

"Is that all?" Toa asked in his sing-song voice.

Scowling, I drew in more until the prickles turned into needles, stabbing my skin and yanking at my hair follicles. "Any more and I'll have to use Stefan—the Boss, I mean—as an overflow."

Toa turned his unwavering stare at Stefan, analyzing him for a few moments before saying, "Show me."

"You might save that for last," Stefan said in a voice filled with steadfast command. "We've only done it once and she did, in fact, pass out. It was an unavoidable risk to both of us."

Toa stared for a few more seconds, causing my butt to tingle in uneasiness. Something was happening. I had no idea what, but judging by my telltale sign of danger near, I stood in a battlefield of some sort.

"Leave it, Toa," Dominicous ordered, his eyes on me. "He is responding like a male to his mate. We'll deal with it after we assess…the matters at hand."

My body filled with warm fuzzies before I could force them away. Holding a crap load of power like a washer woman would a basket of laundry and three squirming kids took all my concentration. I met Toa's stare again and cringed when he said, "Release it."

"Can you open a window?"

I got him to blink! I must've confused him.

"I don't want to blow anything up. It's sometimes easier to just shoot it out a window… Although, someone would have to go kill whatever crops up."

Toa put his hands out in front of him, palms facing each other, and said, "Do this."

I felt a swirl in the air, like static electricity fizzing along my skin. If I was in a thunder storm, I'd look skyward, wondering if a bolt of lightning was about to strike me. Him drawing power? It must be, though I'd never felt anyone else do it, including Stefan. Which was weird, since Stefan and I had that link.

Between Toa's hands glowed a lovely white ball, so white and pure it looked solid. With all the magic filling me, I could make out the tiny fissure marks where the magic didn't gel into the spell perfectly. As I watched, the lines became cracks, which became holes, until the whole thing kind of vibrated into nothing. The magic swooshed back around me.

"Weird." Sweat beading on my brow from holding my max magic for so long, I did as he had done, putting my palms together in front of me and creating something like a tube to direct the magic from my body into the air between my hands.

All hell broke loose.

The magic exploded from my body, knocking into Toa like a solid mass and flinging him backward, his lovely locks flying as haphazardly as his limbs. Stefan had a burnished gold shield in front of him, worried that might happen, and Dominicous had a grin and a new hairdo.

"At least it was benign," Dominicous said with a chuckle, smoothing his hair.

Toa was not amused. Gliding back in front of me like a fallen angle with a vendetta, he squared off with that icy stare once again. "Your control needs work. I need to see the color of your power."

"That almost sounds scandalous," I muttered. "Okay, I think I can make one of those protective boxes—it worked when I didn't want it to, when we battled that caped idiot. It might blow up, though. Oh—I can turn my blade black..."

Toa shook his head. "The coloring is marred by the blade. That is the chief reason for the power-level confusion."

I stuck out my lips in the strange "thinking pout" I was known for. And made fun of. "O-kay, let's see."

"Can you not do spells or charms?" Dominicous asked with disapproval.

"I can attempt a great many spells and charms, but they always turn into something unexpected and usually not very fun."

Dominicous leaned forward. "Show me."

I scanned the room. It housed the usual finery; expensive oil paintings, porcelain knick-knacks, quality and plush furniture. "Probably not wise right here. We should go outside. And you guys will want your swords."

As we exited the room, Charles jumped up with a men-at-arms kind of blank expression. Seeing me, his brow furrowed.

"What ha—?□ His gaze swept to my followers. He peeled away to the side without another word.

I marched forward, anxiety-ridden, knowing in another three minutes I'd make a boob of myself and probably embarrass Stefan. There was nothing for it, though. I just wasn't getting this magic stuff. My spells never worked out how I planned, no matter what level of power I used. I could swing a sword decked in magic, but more often than not it blasted magic out the business end like some Sci-Fi movie.

I stopped about one hundred yards away from the mansion in the backyard. If I was supposed to use black, I needed a lot of room to work with. "Okay, let's aim for something not too…cumbersome."

"Oh, no, I would prefer the gamut, actually," Dominicous said softly.

I turned to him with a new scowl. "What do you mean by, *the gamut*?"

"Give me a sampling, if you please. I want to see how you both cast, and then deal with your problems."

I shook my head. "I don't deal with the problems. Usually I run, and Charles and Adnan, or someone else that knows what they're doing, deal with it."

"Well, then, a little practice for Stefan and me."

Stefan's eyes left me for a second to take in Dominicous. He gave a nod that seemed to act as a bow.

I took a large breath. "Okay, here we go."

I opened up to draw in the elements when I felt a presence beside me. Toa stood nearly arm-to-arm, staring at me across his body.

"I need to monitor how you control the power," he said in reply to my raised eyebrows.

"So, I'm not great at this. A little room to maneuver would help..."

"Battle leaves you no room to maneuver."

"Dealing with that stare is a battle all right..." I muttered grumpily.

Take two.

I drew a perfect balance of elements, mixing them around just so, and then paused. "Should I do black, or a different color?"

"Can you work in other powers?" Toa asked softly.

"Speaking so I can barely hear you doesn't make you any less in my space. And yes, I can work in all other powers, but not very well."

"The gamut," I heard behind me.

I had no end of sighs for this whole experiment. "Brace yourselves."

I tried to focus a binding spell at a dead tree in a lovely shade of blood red, my default. As expected, the tree burst at the base of the trunk, the top crashing down toward us.

"Run!" I yelled, already having started moving with the initial blast.

The procession scattered, a crowd having shown up when we got outside. Two guys got confused on which way to run and kinda shuffled back and forth with their arms out and their eyes wide while the branches fell on top of them.

"That's why they aren't in the Watch." Charles chuckled as he climbed over the crackly dead limbs, trying to fish the two guys out.

"Okay, next." I took a step down in power level, knowing it would show as green. I tried to work an informative spell, which could be left behind so someone treading in your footsteps would alert you with a vibration in your chest. Apparently. I could do it about half the time, and it gave me a shock so bad my teeth chattered.

I mentally called up the chants, not knowing the sounds but understanding the working of power—which seemed to amount to the same thing with me—and moved my hands as though I lay a blanket of feathers on the ground. The green smoke sparkled for a brief second before settling.

I took a giant step back, dragging Toa with me. "Sometimes it shoots fireworks.

Pretty, but be ready with water because it's been known to set things on fire."

Nothing happened.

"Shit." I braced myself.

Toa stepped forward and waved his foot over the spell. The resulting shock nearly fused my teeth together.

"Stop—it works, it works!" I gasped.

Toa turned back to me quizzically. I knew this because one eyebrow was a millimeter above the other, overlaying that familiar stare. "How long does it take to dissipate?"

"I don't know. I'll show you how I deal with it. Stand well back."

Everyone that had ever shared a class with me jogged backward. Toa once again came to stand by my side. "Here we go, a magic attack block. Supposedly. This one never works. Darla tried to teach it to me to prove some sort of point. Joke was on her."

A thin blue jet arced out from my body, first appearing like a mighty force field. The large, translucent blue shield started to contract the closer it got to ground zero, the blue becoming more and more solid, until finally, it covered the area in which the green spell crouched.

Nothing happened.

"Shit."

"Boss, get up there, quick!" Charles urged, rocking forward on the balls of his feet.

Adnan jumped in front of me, his blade whirling a deep red, as a hive of insects burst from the ground, all a sharp, navy blue.

"They're growers!" Adnan shouted, in his customary ninja attack position.

"It's okay, I got this!" I pushed my palms forward. Purple oozing out in a thick glob, spilling across the ground. The magic rolled and boiled, growing in gooeyness to match the growing of the beetle-like insects. When the two collided—the insects had always started running back at me—the bugs got caught, steam rising from their many legs.

"Okay, Adnan, get in there," Charles shouted, chopping at the bugs, twelve in all, caught in the sticky purple fly trap.

The boys had the bugs cut down with their swords and much stronger power before Stefan or Dominicous could even step up. I sucked in the purple magic, the least power level and therefore not a big deal to reel back in. Although, that stare was back.

"What's up?" I turned to Toa.

"That magic did not dissipate, is that correct? You drew it back, like a yo-yo?"

"Like a yo-yo…yeah, I guess. I can't do it with the higher power levels—it needs to find a home. Or else I need Stefan around to brace me, but otherwise, yeah, I try to suck it back in when it isn't trying to kill me in some horrific way."

"Although, the bugs were making their way back to you…"

"Yeah, they do that. I give them life—accidentally, obviously—and they try to kill me. Ungrateful bastards."

"Yo-yo. Please." He made a large sweeping motion with his hand, indicating I should move on to the next stage. He stepped next to me again.

"Okay, well, now we move into the more serious power levels. Stefan and Dominicous, you might step closer. Things will probably get interesting…"

"Can she do anything right?" I heard to my far right.

The answer was no. I'd cried about that fact on Stefan's chest so many times I couldn't count. I had no idea what I was doing wrong. I could follow the spell exactly, mimicking the teacher or student identically, applying power just the way it was described, and while someone else got a happy little dog that waited by a gate, and then ran to its owner with a magical message of some kind, I got a killer wolf trying to kill me. It wasn't the power level, either. I still got a giant, man-eating dog when I used purple, the lowest level I could possibly use. Stuff just didn't work right for me.

The overall consensus was that my magic was weird because I was human. I had long started to agree, regardless of what Stefan said.

I took a cleansing breath, trying to focus even though that blue-eyed stare could throw the most experienced off track. If the guy would just blink once in a while it wouldn't be so bad. Or else, I dunno, move a finger or something!

"I am going to attempt…oh man, what do I want to attempt?"

I thought for a minute into the quiet of midnight. The darkness permeated my awareness, sifting through my fingers and sliding past my skin. I sucked in power, feeling the glow in my chest and the tingle in my limbs. "No one touch me."

A long delicate pale finger slowly reached into my line of sight and poked my bare arm. A blast of magic burst into Toa's skin. A resounding, bone jarring shock rocked him backward. He made a, "Whooee," sound as he shook his hand.

Not able to help my chuckles, I said, "I told you."

"What just happened?" Dominicous asked, stepping forward and peering around a once again staring Toa.

"She electrified her skin somehow," Toa explained in his musical tone, leaning forward to look at my arm, his hands at his sides. "I've never seen that before. Fascinating. Her magic, or a new spell?"

"How did you do that?" Dominicous asked, suspicious of something.

I shrugged, still trying to think of something to try that wouldn't result in a lot of crushed people. "I feel the darkness around me, and then my chest and limbs get hot. Physically hot, I guess, because whenever someone touches me other than Stefan they get a shock."

Toa's stare found Stefan. "Why aren't you affected?"

He shrugged, heat of a different kind filling our special link. "She calls to me, and I to her. I always thought it was because of that, somehow."

"Proceed," Dominicous said suddenly. "I am eager for this portion of the testing to be over."

"There's more after this?" I whined before I could help myself.

"Are you tired?" Toa asked softly, almost mockingly.

I looked at him in confusion, completely unsure why he insisted on talking at the very lower end of his volume level. He looked back—as usual—but this time his gaze was condescending.

I crinkled my nose. "Just wait and see Mr. Marathon."

"Don't do it, Sasha," Charles warned.

"Yes, do it," Toa challenged.

Fine.

Orange, a step above my default red. It wouldn't hurt for very long.

I drew in a nice, big shot of air, mixed it with fire, added just a touch of earth so it would linger, and summoned up a thickening spell tinged with a furnace flare. The object was to solidify the air around an opponent to slow them down. Mine produced one hell of a shock as it did so. It took a lot of energy to execute, like physically holding someone still that wanted to run, but in this instance, it would be worth it.

I left my hands at my sides, because I didn't need those, and flashed a grin in Toa's direction. "Surprise!" I let the magic settle down onto him.

"Aaaeeeee!" Toa convulsed for three seconds before the orange haze started crackling with white and disintegrated into the harmless air around him.

"Oooh, you're fast at that," I commended, giving him a praising downward smile. It was also my thinking smile. I had no idea how he'd done it.

His stare had some of that left over voltage in it. I raised my hands in surrender, "You told me to!"

"When do Stefan and I get to work?" Dominicous asked smoothly.

"Now. I'm going to try the concealing charm and it always creates monsters. Large, fanged monsters." I drew in my mix of charms, dreading this. I should have used this charm with purple, but I didn't expect those danged beetles. They were hard to catch, and hurt when they tried to gnaw on your leg. After I'd figured out the goo, bugs weren't such a problem, but I'd used up the lowest power in my demonstration so my legs didn't have bite marks.

Six of one, half dozen of the other…

Eyes closed because I knew the feel of the charm, and what happened when I used it, I brought my fingers up and swooshed them back down, as if I were fanning a sheet onto the bed. Gold coated a sapling for a fraction of a second.

Nothing happened.

I groaned. Often, explosions were the safest results to charms and spells gone wrong. As I learned more spells and charms, though, mimicking their application perfectly, I got stranger results.

Always the same results if I did the spell "properly," though. So that had to be something.

"Here you go, boys," Charles said with a grimace. "In three, two, one…"

The sapling started swinging wildly, branches flapping like wings, leaves fluttering. It started to grow, upward, twenty feet in the air. Wider now, a huge root stepping out of the ground like a leg, followed by five more.

"Now's the time to cleave it," Charles counseled. "It only gets angry from here on out."

"You do this often?" Dominicous asked pleasantly, not bothering to watch the tree transform into a heinous creature.

"Unfortunately, yes. It's why I try not to use the higher powers. You'll see what happens when I get to white."

That drew Toa's attention away from the tree-animal, his gaze suspicious. "You can do pure white?"

"Yes, though the effects are…unsettling."

"Is this directly after you take Stefan's blood?"

I thought about it. "I dunno. I never mapped out his offerings."

"But you do take his blood?"

"Yes. And he takes mine. Why? Was that supposed to be a secret?"

"When was the last time you took his?"

I thought back. Then shrugged. "Must be a while now, I don't remember. Stefan, do you—?□

A howl cut me off. The monster was thirty feet tall now with branch-like arms. A hole in the top suggested a mouth, but no teeth. Lucky for the boys.

Even still, I started to back away. This damn thing would come after me, and by the look of it, it'd have a long reach.

"We haven't exchanged blood in the customary month before a visit such as this. She has no taint from me, nor I her." Stefan stood with his neck craned, his face his usual stern leader's mask, analyzing the monster.

Charles walked over, placing himself in front of me. Adnan stood off to the side. A couple of my sword fighting classmates sauntered in, too. They'd all gotten really great at working together.

My God, I sucked at this. My heart sank. Stefan would be lucky if I didn't get kicked out.

"Easy, love," he said in his low, deep voice, turning his back on the monster and facing me. "Have faith in yourself."

I loved him more than words could express for believing in me, even though I couldn't show worse if I possibly tried. I pointed behind him. "It's about done growing. Things are about to get real."

He winked. The man was crazy!

Another howl, and the monster sighted in.

"Here we go!" Charles crouched, sword out, orangey-gold with my help.

A giant tree-trunk leg lifted in the air, smashing down on the ground ten feet ahead of it. People started to scream or groan, moving or running backward. A few people high-tailed it out of there entirely.

"Can you not suck out the magic?" Toa asked over another catastrophic howl.

"I tried that once. I could only get half the magic back in before I got the warning prickles. When I released that bit of magic, I set fire to the whole thing. Which meant a huge bonfire monster chased us around for half the night."

"But the magic came from you…"

"Yes, but as I release it, I'm pretty sure the draw isn't cut off. I think I have to cut off the draw at a certain point, but I don't know how.

No one seems to think that is the right way. But…I don't know, I suck at this."

Another earth quaking step. The monster was indeed heading my way.

Stefan drew his sword, burnished gold, the power right under white. Dominicous drew his. Exact same color. Huh.

"What power do you throw after you take her blood?" Dominicous roared over the thick and low tree groans.

Another step forward, within striking range of the two guys.

They could have been having an idle chat over a cigarette for how concerned they were.

"White tinged with a golden hue. Not quite full white. White's a big step up from gold. Even burnished gold, where I sit. I had no idea."

"Hmm. I am gold with white frost when I take Toa's. Interesting."

"So, it's getting angry now…" Charles counseled. "Just FYI."

And it was. Black mouth gaping, still fangless, the beast howled again, shaking the bones of everyone there. People brandished their swords in shaking hands, just in case.

The monster bent to throw a huge, leafed fist toward Stefan. He danced out of the way, smooth and graceful, perfectly balanced. The bark monster howled in rage, throwing another fist, slamming it into the ground where Dominicous had been a moment before.

Stefan rushed between the stomping feet, aiming for his prey. He slashed at the Achilles heel, then cut through half a leg. Dominicous was at the other leg, following Stefan's example. The next stomp had the monster stumbling, but not falling. The root foot broke off, the beast now using a stumped foot.

"It is an actual tree," Stefan shouted, dodging the leafed fist. He slashed at the wrist, chopping some off before rolling out from beneath the tree's next punch, and then dodging a stomp.

Dominicous jumped, tucking his feet and doing a cool flip. Unfortunately, he landed in the path of an already attacking tree-palm and got knocked to the side. He rolled against the forest floor, kicking up dirt and dust, then hopped to his feet and ran back into the fray, his muscles bunching and releasing.

"I would prefer an axe instead of a sword, I think," Stefan reflected in a hum-drum voice, moving like a boxer within the swinging and thrashing of the tree-monster. He used his hands to rip away bark as often as he used his sword to chip away, debilitating the monster little by little.

Dominicous, for his part, did the same thing, his tattoos glowing alongside Stefan's. His movements were jerky and vicious where Stefan's flowed from one strike to the next in perfect, powerful harmony, but each took down the beast in his own way.

After about ten minutes, both men panting and sweaty, I was able to effectively draw enough power out to render the beast immobile. All that remained in its stead was firewood. Which was a money saver come winter—I informed everyone of that fact.

You're welcome.

Stefan yanked off his shirt and sopped the sweat from his chiseled, handsome face. His body glistened in the faint moonlight, his animal magnetism drawing me to him, having me rubbing my palm up his chest without realizing how I got there.

"Thanks for the workout, love," he said, glancing his lips off of mine. "I needed that. It's been a stressful couple of days."

"Two more power levels to go," Dominicous said, stripping his shirt and wiping the sweat off his own face.

I noticed a long, twisted scar up the side of Dominicous's chest. White lines zigzagged across his back, as if he'd been whipped. He saw me looking, and let me. Battle wounds, or the reason he didn't want to attempt emergence—or *re*-emergence, in his case—into the public eye?

I settled on both. I suddenly knew what he fought for. Which side he was on, and why.

"Which was that, gold?" I asked the growing crowd. "So now white."

"Does this create larger monsters?" Stefan asked with a smirk. "Because now I'm warmed up."

"No," I answered, focusing. "Now I do something a touch more scary. No matter what freaking spell I try, I end up with the same result. I abhor working with white for this reason. Stefan, get ready to catch some magic—otherwise we might stand and blink for an hour before it drifts away."

Another huge breath. I drew power and readied myself, a tear falling down my cheek. I really, really hated this one.

The spell let loose, a blanket of magic so fluffy and white it could have been snow. It solidified onto the ground in front of us, the trees disappearing as if they'd never been there, the sky going blue, the ground turning from lush brown and green to a hard, cracked plain of dirt. Desert as far as the eye could see. Nothingness. Death to any wayward traveler.

I heard gasps and shrieks, watching a giant dinosaur walk toward me from the right. Fear gripped me as I noticed its foot long fangs. As I noticed it, noticing me, I turned toward Stefan, reaching out to him. He stepped closer, his eyes wide in shock, his mouth hanging out.

"What is this?" he asked, his words unsure.

"An illusion. Everyone lives it with me. We can wander around in this place, thinking we are trapped in the desert, and potentially hurt ourselves in real life, which we can't see or feel. If we stay still, the dinosaur takes extremely painful bites from us. If we run…"

"You could die or badly hurt yourself. Why did you never tell me? How did I not know about this?"

"I did it once in class and was forbidden from ever doing it again. Since then, I've tried to work on my own—Charles and Adnan wouldn't leave my side when they knew—to free up using the white power, but… This happens every time. The illusion goes only as far as my magic reaches, obviously, but that's plenty far. On a side note, isn't Toa's stare really irritating?"

"He can hear you, you know—"

"The scaled monster is upon us. What happens now?" Toa interrupted, staring at a jaw full of teeth. If he was worried, he hid it behind that angelic face.

"Well, we get bit. It hurts."

"Can you get yourself out of here?" Toa watched the T-Rex step toward us on those powerful back feet, the mostly useless hands half curled at its chest.

"Nope. Not for about an hour. Then I can draw the magic back out."

"An hour, did you say?" That eyebrow had raised a millimeter again.

"Question: do you change your facial expression during sex?" I asked, sidetracked.

"He does, yes," Dominicous said, stepping to Stefan's and my sides. "Will its bite kill me?"

"No." I hesitated. "Well, it hasn't killed anyone else, so I don't think so."

Dominicous stepped forward, hands waving, right under the T-Rex.

"What are you—? I stared as the huge mouth chomped down on his body, his head completely in the mouth. We heard a muffled scream before the beast straightened up, mouth still closed, leaving Dominicous on the ground.

He looked down at himself and patted his stomach, his face pale. "That was incredibly painful. I am intrigued. How is this possible?"

I pointed, aghast. "Careful, you're going to—

The T-Rex went for a side-hold this time, its teeth clamping down on Dominicous's whole middle half. It ripped its head away, again, as if Dominicous was in his grasp. Being that it wasn't more than an illusion, he stayed put, painfully.

Toa touched my cheek with his long finger, peered into my eyes, and then looked back at the T-Rex. Taking the opposite direction of most cowards, he felt the bite next.

"Ooouueeee," he squealed. It wasn't possible for him to get any paler, but he gave it a try.

"Well, I can't be the only one left out." Stefan let go of my hand, next in line for pain.

"A bunch of idiots," I mumbled, sitting down.

Usually it was an hour of pain. Charles, Adnan, and I took turns, but sometimes, when I snuck out in the middle of the day and tried on my own, I just sat in one place, feeling the bite over and over until the magic dwindled enough that I could get out.

Toa held up both hands, palms toward the sky. I watched in rapture as his eyebrows dipped down his nose.

"What is it?" Dominicous asked, stepping closer.

"It won't let me unravel and disintegrate it. There is flux in power at work here. A strange inverse. A crossing in delivery, maybe."

"Like a frozen computer," I said, nodding. "Yeah, I'm doing something tragically wrong, but I have no idea what. I can *feel* the wrongness, too. It makes my heart hurt. But…" I shrugged.

The dinosaur chomped down toward me, distracted at the last minute by Stefan. Stefan took another bite to keep it from me. I wanted to tell him I loved him. To apologize to him for ruining his chance to have a working mate. I wanted him to cure this weird hurt inside me that the magic had caused. I could do none of those things, because the science experiment wasn't over.

"What happens if nobody moves?" Dominicous asked, analyzing Stefan's resolute face.

"I get bit a lot," I explained.

"May I see?"

"No," Stefan interjected reflexively.

"It's fine." I winked at Stefan. "This isn't my first dance. Clear away and let the miracle that is my suckery happen."

Just like when I was alone, the mystical dinosaur bent to me in a rush, jagged teeth bared. All went dark as its head engulfed me, its teeth clamping down on my waist. Like knives digging into my sides, chest and back simultaneously, I gritted my teeth against the sharp, dizzying pain. When it lifted away, I took a steadying breath. Automatically, I said, "One."

"How many have you taken?"

"Between fifty and sixty in a sitting. About one a minute for an hour. It helps keep time."

"You've endured that pain for—□ Stefan cut off as the image cleared away, Toa having disbanded the spell.

"Yeah, but, let's be honest, guys—there is no way that hurts more than childbirth, and it's only an hour. Right?"

Toa wavered, reaching for Dominicous to brace him. "I will need to think on that. That severely taxed my energy levels. I had not realized it was so dangerous."

"Bet your magic tests never went like this before." I jumped up and rubbed my hands together. "I'm a professional at strange paranoia. Okay, on to black, finally."

I drew once again, sucking in deep, curing the failure of white with the bliss and glory of black. I sighed in relief and eased a protective box into existence, the only spell I'd tried in black lately, knowing that it actually worked. As I'd hoped, a large black box, almost solid, materialized in front of me, capturing air.

"Alas, the one I can do right."

The spectators gasped, leaning forward to look at a square.

"It isn't much, but at least it won't try to kill me." I was tired. I wanted to go lie down, mocking smirk from Toa or no.

Toa and Dominicous approached the box slowly, probably terrified it would grow arms and bite. Dominicous walked around the outside, his arms crossed over his chest. I used the stare-free time to lean against Stefan, closing my eyes when his arms came around my waist. He kissed me on the head and squeezed.

Dominicous reached out a hand to touch the box.

"Don't," I warned. "The shock is worse than when Toa touched me earlier."

He continued reaching.

Like a bug zapper, a life-sized buzzing blared, flinging Dominicous flat on his back. He lay with his arms out, eyes open in shock. Charles wheezed out a laugh he couldn't stop in time.

"Can you get rid of this?" Toa asked, still analyzing the box, easing a dagger from his pocket.

"I think so. Or I can blow it up."

Toa pushed the very tip of a glowing white blade toward the box. As soon as it touched a lesser buzz sounded, having Toa flinching back with a, "Eeeeah!"

"Let's move back into the house, shall we?" Dominicous suggested, hauling himself up slowly. "As men, we love an explosion, but maybe just disengage it, if you can."

I got to work unraveling, something I could do easily with black. If I wasn't terrified of what would happen when the spells went wrong, I'd use black way more often.

Chapter 4

The procession entered the same room we'd been in earlier, but this time Charles was allowed to sit in the corner. I think Stefan and Dominicous had had enough with pain, monsters, and workouts. Not that they would admit it. The way they went about it, Charles was there for moral support.

"We now need to test your human vulnerabilities," Dominicous started, sitting gratefully. "If you are to be mage, like Stefan hopes, you have to withstand our influences. Our pheromones."

Stefan tensed slightly but said nothing. I just nodded. I'd been through this with Luke, the clan's best at mental manipulation. I'd gotten turned on for a second, I'd gotten a quick dose of fear, and I'd gotten pissed when he touched my boob. He hadn't been expecting the slap.

Toa drifted in front of me, his appearance like one fresh out of the powder room. If I hadn't just seen him electrocuted, thrown around the dirt, chased in a clearing, and shocked, I would've suspected he'd just arrived at the mansion. Amazing.

"You can close your eyes or keep them open, as it befits you." Toa waited for me to nod.

He knew humans.

A tingling erupted at the bottom of my sternum. The flight reflex. He was trying fear first.

My limbs got jittery and my breath shallow. My body tensed.

My first impulse was to reach for my dagger. A huge smile erupted on my face and I stared at Toa manically, daring him to try anything. I even had my rape whistle handy—he didn't know what he was messing with!

Then I took a big breath and forced it all away. Stefan could do that with just a look, usually when he wasn't even trying. Something would irritate him, or I would put myself in danger somehow, and his face would contort into a severe mask that had my heart beating and my butt tingling. He didn't need the pheromones. Through stubborn practice, I'd gotten used to ignoring it.

Toa blinked twice, straightening up. If I looked really hard, I swear I could see a faint flush. *Swear* I could.

"Next," Dominicous prompted.

A haze swept over me, clouding my awareness and almost my vision. I hated it. It made me feel lost and dizzy, and I hated both of those sensations. It's why I never took up smoking.

I drew in a blast of power and wiped the thought away, finding a lingering presence at the outside of my skull where Toa lurked. I soaked into it, and then applied fire, blasting it open.

Toa staggered back, his eyes wide.

"I gave him an expression!" I giggled. It was the small things.

"What happened?" Dominicous said, appearing on the edge of his seat without his body actually moving. Eyes like the gleaming edge of a blade, he was ready to fight, but still seemingly lounging in the chair. Neat.

Also, awful. And scary. He didn't need the pheromones to manipulate fear, either.

"She broke my attempt. Like shattering the overlay on her mind. Full of surprises, this one. She shouldn't have been allowed to exist so long without training. But then, she has developed some truly spectacular defenses. I'd like to see her in a foreign place. I have a feeling she could develop many lost treasures."

"Try to cut off my magic," I blurted. I wanted to see if the little ditty I'd just done would work on that.

"All in due time," Toa replied noncommittally.

My body erupted in goose bumps, shivers of delight working up from my groin. My face flushed and my skin started to tingle. Wow, it felt *good*. Like I wanted to reach out and touch the smooth sex trap in front of me. It reminded me of when I'd first met Charles and my brain went on complete hiatus despite the setting. That level of coercion I'd long since been able to block. But Mr. Toa-man had some tricks up his sleeve. He gave it to me much harder, breaking through my already practiced blocks.

It wasn't him I wanted, though.

My gaze slid across his almost too perfect face and sought those deep, dark eyes of the man I loved. I wanted to rip his clothes off and take him right now, these people be damned. He sat across the room, a twinkle in his eyes, his bulge pronounced and ready. Fire shot through our link, fizzling up my body and nearly overtaking me. I focused on that earth-shattering face, rugged and handsome, an appearance to give any fabled vampire a run for their money.

I heard a throat clear.

"I think she has gotten off track," Dominicous said lightly. "What an unusual smell. Like…fallen leaves on the lush forest floor. Vibrant and alive."

Stefan winked, pride welling up in our link. I'd still chosen him even though the pheromones were supposed to direct me toward Toa.

Silly man. Of *course* I'd choose him! Who wouldn't?

"I'd like to see this overflow you two speak of," Dominicous said as I pulled my gaze away from Stefan.

"Until I pass out, or just enough to stay conscious?" I clarified. "I'm no stranger to magic shock, but I'm also no stranger to nearly dying from it. So…"

"Conscious would be best, if at all possible." Dominicous hid a smirk.

Hmph.

I drew in, filled up, and felt the warning prickles. *Here we go.* I kept on going, letting more gush in. Past a healthy dose and on, to the red line. More still. When my vision got hazy I opened the link and let Stefan siphon off whatever he could hold. A lovely white-gold sparkling arch of magic bloomed in the room. It's use? I had no idea, but it sure was pretty.

Obviously I didn't create it. Otherwise it might have tried to eat somebody.

"Again, Sasha, but steal the magic this time. Not all, but enough to get your point across and stay on your feet," Stefan commanded lightly.

Righty-o. He apparently thought I was a master at this stuff.

I tried to remember how I did it the first time—I didn't just pull elements; I focused on the others in the room. Then, because I couldn't grasp the magic they held—since they held it within themselves—I envisioned them trying to hurt Stefan. Trying to direct an attack as Trek had done. As if I pulled a string from their bodies, I slowly emptied not only the room, but them, of magic.

The warning came in a rush this time, threatening to overwhelm me. Pain lanced my body, my inner alarm blaring. I felt Stefan tug on the link, taking magic from my body, trying to balance me, but there was too much. Toa could hold a bit more than Trek. Dominicous could hold as much as Stefan. All in all, too much!

The flood drowned me, dumped over my head and suffocated me. I felt consciousness leaving, like I had at that battle. More magic siphoned out, but even more dumped in.

I threw my palms out. Black exploded into the room, turned the air sluggish, and then thick. Then solid. Everyone froze, not because they wanted to, but because I'd just—somehow—successfully executed the thickening spell. *Really* executed it, too. The only person that could move was me.

Alarm pulsed through the link. Stefan stared at me, unable to even talk because he couldn't move his jaw.

"So, shit. Lemme…shit!" I thought really hard. I'd never been able to do it, so I didn't know how to undo it.

I sprinted for the door, but couldn't rip it open because of the damn air. "Crap!"

I sprinted in the other direction, diving through the open window like James Bond, and then running so fast around the giant mansion that my legs didn't feel like my own. I hammered down the hallway, burst through two doors, straight armed a naked dude advancing on a waiting woman wearing a blindfold, and catapulted into the correct corridor. A team of attack-dog looking men waited outside of the room I was just in. Harsh and well-trained, they were supposed to be guarding against any foul play.

They weren't doing a real bang-up job!

"Anybody know how to break or stop a thickening spell?" I gasped, my sides heaving as I gulped air.

A whole defense team of eyes turned my way. There was an awkward beat while they placed my face and comprehended my words, and then they were active. Just not in the way I had hoped.

Three guys reached for me immediately. I dodged out of the way and ducked under another pair of giant, groping hands. I backed against the wall and threw a protective spell around myself, not knowing any other way to keep them off while getting very important information.

Three sets of hands kept reaching for me, apparently overconfident in their invincibility. A loud buzzing flung them away from my self-made cage.

"So, anyway, I need help undoing a spell…" I said in a rush.

A six-and-a-half foot block of muscle stepped in front of me. "Where is the Regional?"

"He's in the room still, locked in place because I turned the air solid. I need to undo that. *Quickly.* I'm pretty sure they can breathe, but if they can't, we don't have much time!"

The man stared at me for a second. If I hadn't grown used to Toa, it would have disconcerted me. He turned to someone behind him. "Break open the door."

"Best to try and rip it out. Air's solid. It's not going in…" I reminded, and then shrank against the wall as the flat-eyed stare of the large guy turned back to me.

"How did you turn the air solid?" he asked, his deep voice thundering out of his chest.

"Uh…with a spell…" I grimaced in a hopeful sort of way.

Through the link, Stefan's alarm had turned into bemused patience. The man dealt with a lot where it concerned me, and when in private, it tickled him to no end. I had no idea why, because I even flabbergasted myself. But at least he could breathe. That was the main thing.

"Show me," the guard said.

"You've *got* to be kidding." I shook my head as the first guard tried to bust down the door. Obviously it didn't go into the room, but it did splinter. The wooden shards were pulled away, revealing a room with three men as still as the grave, all except their eyes. Charles, probably wishing he *hadn't* been put in the room, was most probably still in his corner, and out of view.

I waited behind my shield, watching each man try to force their way into the room. "Good spell, though," I mused. "Kind of tiring, though. That one could definitely come in handy down the road, I think."

"Undo this," the head guard said to me. Not too bright, this guy.

"Yeah, I would love to. Which is exactly why I had to go through the window and come around here. I have no idea how."

"Undo what you did. Reverse it!"

Toa started to loudly hum in that way a person does when their mouth was gagged but they had important information to impart. I moved to the end of my protective bubble and peered in the room, just making out his wide eyes.

"I don't think that's a good idea. Toa seems perturbed."

"Then how do we undo it?" the head guard asked.

It was like I hadn't run up in a dead sprint a few minutes ago asking that very same question. "Possibly find a teacher of mine to lend a hand?"

Toa started to do his communicatory hum again.

"Maybe not. He's probably afraid I'll blow them up."

An hour later I sat in my bubble, cross-legged on the ground, my chin on my fists, watching as white power zipped around the room. My magic had receded, and while the men couldn't move much, they could move enough for Toa to get his palms and magic active. I was plenty able to suck the residual magic out of the room now, and I suspected

Stefan could've as well, using that weird balancing thing he did, but the humor dancing in his eyes as Toa stubbornly tried to undo whatever I had done, kept me from mentioning it.

Finally, in a bright flare, I felt a tug on my chest. All captured men took a huge, lung-filling breath.

"Okay, come out of there." The head guard, whose name was Bernie, jerked his hand in the air to facilitate my removal.

"Nope. I think I'll just hang on to see if they're angry."

"Your magic fades. You'll have to come out sometime."

"Wrong again. I keep replenishing this spell. Or charm. You know, I have no idea what the difference is. At any rate, this baby is as strong as strong can be. I'm good in here for a little longer."

Unfortunately, a little longer wasn't long at all.

One very serious-looking Regional strolled up to my self-made cage and looked down on me. His perfectly blank face still managed to communicate his complete lack of humor at that moment. "Care to enlighten us on what happened?"

That stare had me babbling. "Too much power filled me too quickly and I had to do something with it! For some reason I did that thickening spell. But then I didn't know how to undo it because I'd never successfully done it before. But I couldn't open the door because the air was, well, you know how it was. So I ran around the side, but then your guards thought I did something awful—which doesn't really make sense since I ran back toward them—so I locked myself in here for protection until we could figure it out!"

"You tried that spell outside and couldn't complete it. Why did it work this time?"

"I have no idea!"

And I didn't. Largely, everything to do with magic had thus far eluded me. School had never been my strong suit. My magic not working properly meant I hadn't been able to figure it out.

"She has been working with lesser levels of power in the wrong way," Toa explained, leaning against the walls. "She could have great control, but first needs to learn the ways of directing her power. It is like riding a bicycle extremely slow. The bicycle wobbles; balance is hard to maintain. Ride it with more speed, and you will steer with ease."

Toa could learn a thing or two from Dominicous's stare.

"I see. I am not in the habit of sitting, for an hour, in extremely uncomfortable situations."

"Sorry," I mumbled.

He grunted. Apparently an apology had been his agenda. After the explanation, obviously.

He turned to Stefan. "We'll need another room. I'd like to wrap this up and make plans for the next steps."

"There's more?" I asked in horror.

"Not for you. Please wait in your chambers until you are called. You are excused."

After glancing toward Stefan and seeing I wasn't in any danger, I picked apart my protective shield and went on my way. Charles did not follow.

*****

"Toa, results please," Dominicous asked with a straight back, sitting in a leather chair.

They'd moved to a room in the back of the mansion and warded the room against eavesdroppers. They each sat in separate chairs, trying to mask the importance of these findings, both for Stefan, and for their overall cause. Finding someone with a black power level could open doors they hadn't even contemplated.

Stefan had another reason to be nervous, as well. They would need to discuss his mate, and his future. Most importantly, what would happen if those two things couldn't both be Sasha while in his leadership role.

"Her power is beyond my own," Toa said easily. "It doesn't work like mine, either—like ours. She is like a conductor for magic. Like a hub. She doesn't have to reach for it and pull it into herself, she merely has to identify which elements to let in, and then try to stop the flow once she has begun to draw. Her spells will continue building magic until realized, always trying to return back to her. As you saw, her spells, once laid, take longer to unravel. And like you saw, that is not always a good thing."

"Then...she is definitely black," Dominicous clarified.

Stefan held his breath.

"Without a doubt, she is a myth reincarnate. And completely, *completely* ignorant as to the ways magic works. All the training she's received thus far is useless. She blows things up because she is the polar opposite to my—our people's—power. She tries to work a spell inverted, and it combusts."

Stefan let his breath out in a slow exhale. He couldn't say he wasn't relieved. "Odd for a human to wield black, though."

"Not at all," Toa waved him away like a pauper at a king's table. "She is the polar opposite *because* she is human. You are familiar with the yin-yang sign. That was originally created as a representation of the union of the different sides of magic. White and black magic working together is the strongest cohesive bond in the world. White magic is also a scale. As is black. She is at the higher end of the scale; I am at the middle of white. The black power has always been wielded by a human, the white by us. That is why it is so intensely rare. Not rare to possess—not any more than white—but rare to find. One in a million. Humans have power, but so rarely seen because so few believe. And also because we…have our own prejudices.

"At the top of the scale, and acting as a hub, which is rare in itself—not because she is human, but in general—it is like trying to swim in the ocean in the middle of a hurricane. Magic is wild, and forcing into her like it does, makes the wielder constantly fight for control—even in someone experienced. Mistakes can easily be fatal. Because of this—that is speculation—she has developed some sort of rough control directly tied to survival. Living untrained for so long, she has learned to coexist. Now, however, seeing how she is supposed to work with it, the danger becomes more grave. Her ability to take in magic more extreme."

"You see, Toa, she was fated to live," Dominicous said in a smug sort of way.

Stefan barely had time to wonder at that comment when Toa snorted. "One in a million. The odds are incredible, but here she is. What next?"

Dominicous turned to Stefan. "You plan to mate her, is that right?"

A thrill went down Stefan's back. Without hesitation, he answered, "Yes."

"Like her power level, mating between kinds has turned into myth. At least with someone of your stature and position. Your people must approve in order to grant her that title. If she cannot lead, she is useless, and therefore cannot mate you. It is twisted, you see."

Stefan nodded.

"I understand your enthusiasm, of course," Dominicous went on. "She is your one true mate. She needs your power and special ability balancing the wildness of it, and you gain and exult from hers. You two sync. That is plain to see. If you can work in tandem, you could create an exponentially dynamic team. You have linked with her already, you have marked her…and you are in luck on a couple of scores. One, she is a *seer*. Or, more probably, has *seer* blood. That is the reason for the smell she has when aroused. Or, I should say, that is the side-effect. There are other smells, but mostly females exude them. It doesn't seem as though she has many female friends within this group…"

Stefan shook his head to the question as he asked, "*Seer?*" He'd never heard of such a thing.

"Humans have this trait in large doses. Many become psychics or readers of some kind, some even ghost hunters—even though that is a different talent. Some just think it is female intuition or, for a man, a shot of ego. Regardless, she has some sort of partial ability on that score. That secures her as a justifiable lineage for mating, besides the huge blessing in magical power, of course."

"Why are you helping me? I would've thought you'd resist a human as my mate. Possibly even try to take her with you back to the Council for training within the folds of political power."

"Why am I helping you?" Dominicous asked. "That is simple. She is my kindred."

After a long pause, Stefan said, "Come again?"

Chapter 5

I sat facing the woods on a wooden bench just behind the mansion's back door. For the last half hour Stefan had blasted incredulity through the link, then suspicion, then mistrust. Finally, resignation. I knew it had to be about me. What else could it be? I could be hopelessly narcissistic at times, especially while hopeful in a dress, but I didn't think this was a case of fashion-itis.

I felt his presence come up behind me, then around, sitting next to me on the stone bench. I leaned into his great, muscled shoulder, feeling solidity and strength.

"I just had a very…interesting meeting," he started, roping an equally great arm around my shoulders.

I closed my eyes as a delicate wind caressed my face in passing. The night sky had lightened, swishing its metaphorical cape to *olé* the daylight through. The familiar magic soaked into my skin, my chest and limbs warming.

"Hmm," Stefan said, squeezing me. He could feel it as I could. However his special gift worked, it enabled him to share in the feeling, his skin electrifying, as mine did to outsiders. But within our embrace, only pleasure pulsed between our bodies. We sat outside often, sharing the night with each other.

"You are a *seer,* did you know?" he asked quietly.

"As in, like, a fortune teller?"

"Yes." He shrugged. "I guess. In full strength a person can see the future before it happens. Can you do that?"

"No. But I do get, like, premonitions. Kind of…I don't know. Like a directional sense. It's how I find your secret doors."

He shook his head. "That sounds like your magic. What about when you battled Jonas? You seemed to move right before he got there…"

I thought back. I'd had a letter opener and a whistle as my only defense to rescue my ex-boyfriend Jared from a sadist named Jonas. Oh, yeah, I remembered. Stefan was right, I had moved just in time.

"I don't know. Maybe a *seer*, or maybe my survival instinct, or maybe just female intuition."

"Apparently female intuition is a mark of a *seer.* I am led to believe more than a few humans have this trait."

"Ah. And how did you know I had this?"

"That smell you give when you're aroused. Arousal has to come naturally, however. Since we are rarely without the pheromones when dealing with humans, manipulating their lust or some other emotion, well…"

That wasn't the cause for concern. The shoe had yet to drop.

"You have to go away," he said.

And there it was. I turned my face into his shoulder. "Without you, I take it."

"Yes, but only for a short time. Dominicous is sending you and Toa into the *Mata* territory as some sort of…exchange program. You will go as a delegation. As my mate."

My body froze, a tear nearly wobbling free from the first piece of news. I straightened up slowly, my eyes meeting his. I could just make out his perfect face in the shadow, breathtaking as always, but with a slow smile and softening of eyes that he wouldn't show in public.

"I love you."

It was the first thing that came to me.

He leaned over slowly, brushing his lips with mine. "I love you, too. I know a human tradition is to ask for your hand with jewelry and surprise and all that, and I will do that for you, but this exchange is, unfortunately, business."

I shook my head, tears at the surface for a different reason. "You don't need to."

He nibbled my lips, softly brushing them with his tongue, but backed off before I could deepen it. "Your status as my mate is my intention. It is not cemented, unfortunately. My clan has to accept you as co-leader. Which means you actually need to learn to lead." He smiled at me in jest. "Dominicous thinks it is wise to train you away from prying eyes.

"This progression is important, and your status as human and my mate is important. You are very much one of us, but also human. You cross that line. We hope…" He paused, a vein popping out on his jaw from how hard his jaw clenched.

I nudged him with a grin.

"I am *supposed* to hope," he amended, "that you develop a positive relationship with them. To unite our two factions."

"Who are these *Meta?"*

"*Mata.* Shape Changers. Varmints and critters and useless fools that think I should make way for their strange rituals and odd behavior."

"I'm sorry—□ I leaned forward to think for a second. I turned to him on the bench, needing to be absolutely clear about this. "Shape Changers? As in…werewolves?"

"Yes, and no. Well, not really. There are wolves—the stinky, mangy animals. But also other absurd human mutations."

"Okay, I am getting the feeling that you don't like these people—□

"Mata."

"—but I am stuck on the 'turning into an animal' part of the story. How is that *real?"*

"I'll let them explain it. There is one other thing. Who are your parents?"

That took me aback. "Because of the lineage thing? I don't know. I lost them when I was five years old in a multiple car accident. I told you that, remember?"

"But you survived."

"Yes. I was found a mile away in a park sitting on my own. Do you not listen to me?"

"And you have no idea how you got there?"

I shook my head, returning Stefan's intense gaze. "Why?"

"Dominicous. He…is claiming you as his."

Two emotions warred through me. One was an intense confusion, because since I first walked into the room with him, I'd felt something. It was very faint, almost a non-thing, but…it was vaguely familiar. Like I'd known him all my life.

The next was a thrill of fear, dropping my jaw. "So you had to challenge him, or whatever? Because I am not sleeping with that man!"

Stefan chuckled, and then looked around to make sure the big bad leader wasn't caught actually laughing. We wouldn't want a mass challenge because he had a sense of humor…

"He put you in that park. He saw you that night, a little girl standing amongst the carnage, flame starting to lick up your leg. He removed you, fed you his blood to ensure you lived until found, and then waited until you were. He's as close to a father as you have. He has put himself in that role. I'm sure your power level helped solidify his decision regarding this."

My world tilted and reeled. Then fell over.

A huge chunk of my life had just surfaced. The last piece that helped me put it all in perspective.

I had always been able to see the shadow men and women lurking in the night, huge people no one else had noticed. I could sense their presence, knowing I shared the world with something else, but never able to identify it with a likeminded person. Strange events had mentally crippled others, but energized me. I rushed into scuffles and battles where others, like Jared, whimpered.

"Would his blood have any lasting effect?" I asked in a daze.

Stefan pulled me into his body, sensing my strangeness to this news. "We don't know. Trauma is a funny thing, especially to a child. But you resist our pheromones easily, and you have a soft link to him, though the experiences of the day have probably masked that. He thinks of you as blood, since he gave you blood as a child. Usually, giving blood once isn't enough for any sort of lasting link."

"But maybe to a child…"

Stefan gave a noncommittal shrug.

"So…what does that mean?" I asked.

"It means lineage is the least of your worries. So is a backer. That will help bring people around. All you have to do is learn to lead. Learn to hold your cards to your chest, and most importantly, learn to defend yourself. As my mate and especially bearing my mark, any battles you have are also my battles. Unfortunately, that reverses, as well. If I am challenged, you will be expected to meet that challenge with me."

"Well, I'm pretty good at protective boxes and freezing air…"

He chuckled, rubbing my back. "Yes, very. If they'd had any doubt to your power level, that took it away. Toa has not recovered. He's not used to someone with a higher power level that is not sitting on a council somewhere."

I closed my eyes as his soft lips trailed up my neck. "Shall we head to bed?"

"No time. I need you." His teeth barely scraped against my suddenly throbbing pulse.

I gasped, my stomach doing a somersault.

"Hmm, freshly baked cookies on a warm summer evening."

I had yet to ask him about his parents, forever curious how they had died, but never sure how to bring it up and chickening out. Once again, this wasn't the time.

I let my head fall back as he kissed down my chest, getting to my cleavage, and then unzipping my hoodie. His hands tucked under my thin shirt, lightly trailing along my stomach as his mouth took in my ear lobe. I felt him undo the top button of my pants.

"Oh!" A thrill shot through me, a possible witness making my panties go wet.

I kissed Stefan harder, wanting to try this. Wanting to act like his people and express myself openly. Wanting to engage in sexual expression outdoors! In plain sight!

Embarrassment and social rules reared their head. *Oh, my God, am I seriously going to do this?*

"We'll go fast, love. Like getting into cold water," Stefan assured me, his lips quirking.

He knew I wanted to experiment. That I wanted to try some kinky things in an extremely safe and trusting situation. But oh, Lord…

I jumped up and ripped off my pants, trying to get my panties off as well, but was stopped by his hands.

"Hold on just a moment."

He bent forward, his fingers peeling off the lace of my underwear as his face dipped between my legs. I moaned and closed my eyes, all thought slipping away as his naughty tongue hit me in just the right places. My body started to burn as the pressure increased, shivers erupting from my groin and spiraling up my torso.

He backed off, his eyes holding mine hungrily. "I love you," he said as he undid his pants and slipped them down his muscular thighs. His erection sprung free, large and bobbing.

He took my hand and brought me closer, lifting my legs to each side of him, allowing me to kneel on the bench and position my body over his. His tip pushed past my lips slowly until he had sheathed himself completely, filling me up.

I hugged him, showing him my throat, craving that deeper connection. The scrape of his tooth exhilarated me, offsetting the sweet rush of him inside my body. Pain, like pinching, blossomed at the base of my neck. My gasp immediately turned into a moan; his suction reached all the way through my body, tingling my groin as he dove in and out, the pleasure from the contrast something I could barely comprehend with sensations so complex.

I rocked harder, my body feeling that pull, then the wet slide, tingles overcoming me. I sucked in magic, fire and air mostly, the others swirling in, too, and poured it into his body along with my essence, wanting to share myself with him in this new, magical way.

With each pull my chest grew hotter, my limbs humming, the connection with him deep inside me exploding. Stefan moaned, his lips still at my throat, thrusting into me as I pounded down on him. The pressure mounted, at a crest now, so tight.

"Oh, *G—od!*" I cried, blasting apart, the very seams of my being coming undone.

Stefan shuddered into me a second later, hugging me with ragged breaths. He leaned against my chest, his ear to my heart. "Lovely."

"That was fun," I murmured contentedly, draping across him. "Let's go to sleep. It's been a long day."

Fifteen minutes later we walked down the hall toward his room, only to find Charles sitting outside. "Hey, Boss, Sasha. Heard about the trip, wanted to talk to you—□

Charles squinted at Stefan. "Sasha, step away for a quick sec, would you?"

I took one step, my hand still in Stefan's.

"Boss…you… Sasha, go another step. Actually, go in the room for a second."

"What's the matter?" Stefan asked in a deep growl.

Charles put up his hands immediately. "Did she mark you, somehow? Can humans do that? You know what, you two have issues, that's all I'm saying."

Stefan stared at him.

"I'm stepping out of line, and I know it," Charles continued, "But Jonas guarding her on this trip is a terrible idea. He can't be trusted. He said something about other plans before you banished him for a time. Just a thought, but that's a weird coincidence, you know? So, he has got to be a no-go. I can protect her, along with Snow White."

"Go to bed, Charles, before you say something you can't unsay," I said quietly, watching the edge creep quickly into Stefan's eyes.

"Yeah, good call. I want a day off. Also, good night." Charles trudged away, the least graceful I had ever seen him.

"He had his legs crossed when you froze us all. His balls got extremely hot and sweaty in that hour." Stefan chuckled as we walked into his section of the mansion. "I felt bad for the guy."

"He deals with a lot around me," I said sadly. "I love having him around—he's like a brother to me—but maybe you should rotate him out. He's got to be sick of the bodyguard detail."

Stefan sighed and unceremoniously stripped. "I'll talk to him about it. For now, though, I'm exhausted." He reached for me, folding me within his strong arms, then sighed gratefully. "G'night, mate."

I didn't mention that he sounded Australian.

*****

"You are worried."

Stefan glanced at Dominicous on his right before returning to the final preparations in front of him. It had been a short two weeks since Dominicous and Toa showed up, but the Regional had lost no time. Today the delegates left to visit and make repairs with the largest nuisance in the history of the world: those damn Shape Changers. Stefan would ban them all from his side of the world if he could.

The whole lot of them would rather run and hide than stick their neck out for Stefan's kind. He'd seen it often enough, and histories had shown it more than that. To think that now he would stick out his hand to welcome these miscreants into his fold, when he knew they'd just turn tail and sprint away at the first sign of danger, galled.

"Worried is not a term I know," Stefan answered, an eye always on Sasha.

He not only had to make social repairs, he had to send a piece of himself—the largest, most important piece of himself—into their den. If they turned tail, they'd leave her behind. And then Stefan would kill them all.

Dominicous laughed, easily ignoring the violence sweating out of Stefan's every pore. "I am sending Toa. He is the best magic worker of his age, and soon to be one of the top three in the world. He will see her safe from the enemy. From herself, though, that is a different concern."

Stefan clenched his jaw, a bad trait that showed weakness.

"In other news," Dominicous went on good-naturedly, "it seems she has found a way to mark you, though she is human and shouldn't have the capability. Such an interesting female. Survival is strong in her. You should have seen her that night, stumbling away from the wreckage, and then staring down a hunting party. Usually I wouldn't get involved, but… well, here we are."

"She doesn't have the dumb luck of youth anymore. She has a complex to save those close to her. If she makes friends with those... with the *Mata*, then she'll risk her life to save their cowardly hides."

"Noble."

"Foolish."

Dominicous bowed his head. "Here is Tim now."

A stocky male of average human height with a barrel chest walked up as if he expected an attack at any moment. His brown eyes flashed in his grim face, in a clear attempt to appear forbidding.

Stefan would show this shifter forbidding...

"Tim," Dominicous said easily, stepping forward to deliver a human handshake. "You know of Stefan, of course."

Tim's eyes snapped to Stefan's. The hard gaze tried for intimidating. Stefan almost laughed.

"I do," the mongrel stated.

Stefan stuck out his hand, as was right in his role, for the human handshake. The man met the grip, squeezed, then stepped away, out of Stefan's reach. Smart.

"Let's move past the pleasantries, shall we?" Dominicous asked easily. "Tim, you have some valuable possessions being transferred into your care. That is the reason for their guard. They are both extremely high in magic, but one, Sasha, is untrained. Our enemy seeks

Sasha as a poor miner seeks gold. She needs to train, but most importantly, she needs to be kept well away from enemy lines. We have leaks in our establishment, which means they will probably know she goes with you. Which is why her exact destination is solely in your hands."

Dominicous paused for a second, his gaze sweeping toward Toa, who had directed his trademark stare at Jonas, loading supplies into an off-road vehicle. Jonas, strong, fierce, and resolute, either didn't notice the gaze, or, most likely, was not bothered by it. Jonas had his faults in plenty, but he was loyal. He and Stefan had grown up together, and out of everybody, Jonas knew most why the filthy vermin couldn't be trusted. He'd been there when Stefan had learned firsthand.

His focus returning from his linked mage, Dominicous continued, "We trust you with these most valuable possessions because we want to solidify our agreement. It is a huge leap of faith not only for our organization, but with Stefan and me personally. So, I must warn you, if you treat them ill, or have any dealings with our enemy, I will personally see to it that every one of your people is destroyed. Going a step further, I will personally make it my mission to eradicate your entire race from this earth, starting with the children. I hope you can believe me on that score..."

In a show of pure courage, or absolute stupidity, Tim said, "You forget, those aren't the only…loved ones being exchanged. You have my Beta—my second in command--and his entire family. His wife is pregnant. We each have given over something precious to ensure this working relationship. It is that important, and so we will treat it as such."

"Then we understand each other. I'll leave you to it. Stefan, you might say your goodbyes."

Stefan stared at Tim as Dominicous walked away toward Toa, wanting to verbalize his own threats, but refrained, knowing he'd only sound redundant. Instead, for his mate, he said, "Sasha thinks she fails constantly, which brings her down. I'd be grateful…" Stefan refused to let his jaw clench. "…if you would play positive around her. Keep her spirits up. She is truly a remarkable female, but she doesn't know it."

"In return, I hope you'll keep Esmine comfortable. She is heavily pregnant."

"We cherish pregnant females. She will be well looked after."

Tim stared for a beat before saying, "I know about what happened with your parents. It is a different pack now than it was then. We do not abide by such absolute cowardice. I want you to know that."

Rage welled up in Stefan, barely in check. Sasha looked over in surprise, meeting his eyes with a question. She felt his sudden turmoil and, like the dear heart she was, would leave everyone waiting to come over and check. Dear heart, but terrible leader. Trusting he could work his way out of situations was something she still had to learn.

For the moment, though, he was thankful—not that he could admit it, obviously. Especially in front of a sack of farts like this pack of critters in front of him.

Stefan calmed his mind so his mental trash-talking didn't turn verbal and end the agreement right here. He nodded once, and then strode away.

Chapter 6

I stopped loading the few meager possessions I owned into the car and stuffed my hands in my pockets. I'd never really had a home, which was true. Living with a foster family didn't allow me to get too comfortable putting down roots. Then my small apartment, the first space that became *mine,* had been something like a handout from the city for my parentless status. I paid the rent and didn't get any breaks on rent after a year, but still, I hadn't exactly earned it.

But now, as the door was opened by a solid man with wild eyes, I felt a clump of lead form in my chest. If ever I had a home, this was it. I had my own area in a secret spot, with a standing invitation to treat Stefan's rooms as my own. I had been given leave to decorate as I wished, hang pictures if I wanted, and otherwise have the run of the place. He had invited me in permanently; to share his space, make it mine.

On the cusp of deciding I would like that very much, I was being packed up again and sent on my way. Sure, it wasn't for that long, and yes, I needed to get trained away from spectators, but still, a girl could whine a little.

"Sasha." The voice tingled down my spine and lit me up.

Stefan stood behind me, his eyes intent but soft, his face something from a magazine cover. "This is farewell. I will see you soon. Take care of yourself and come back to me safe, okay? Don't do anything foolish and make sure to stay close to Toa, Charles, or Jonas at all times."

I slid my arms around his neck, letting him hug me close. He backed off enough to kiss me, his lips and manner indulgent, giving me something familiar and solid to hang on to. He didn't rush me or hurry me along for the sake of his gruff leadership role. Instead, his tongue played, chasing mine, intertwining as his hands roamed my body, as if he were feeling and remembering each curve to have something to hold on to when we had to endure our nights away from each other.

"Okay," I said into his chest when my body started to heat up uncomfortably. It wasn't the time for a quickie. "I'll come back ready to lead an army."

He smiled down on me. "I love you."

I took a big breath and wiped a tear. "You'd think I never spent any time alone."

He rested his palm lightly on my cheek. "It feels like we've been together all our lives. Keep your link open and I'll feel you. It'll lessen the distance."

I got a pang of longing as he stepped away. His face smoothed over into his familiar mask of steel as a burly man with a pronounced five o'clock shadow padded up with silent footsteps. He moved like a robust dancer, powerful but sleek. His brown eyes flicked at Stefan before landing on me.

"Sasha," his graveled voice rumbled out of his chest, "My name is Tim. I am the alpha, which means all decisions go through me. We'll have an easy time of it, don't you worry." He stood at the door, silently asking me to get in and get on our way.

I took one last look at Stefan, before I turned toward the car, and right into a staring, blue-eyed creeper. "Gah! *Toa! Je*-sus! Warn a girl when you plan to sneak up behind her."

"You should be sensing for others with your magic. I should not be able to sneak," Toa replied with silky patience.

I shook my head and climbed into the car.

"Your lessons have officially begun," Toa said before the car had even started moving. "First we shall go over the principles of magic, starting with the elements. Now…"

My thoughts drifted sideways, Toa's musical voice droning on as the city flashed by. I was interested to learn more about the *Mata*, wondering if they lined up with what I'd heard in stories, or if they, too, had a different twist on reality. I assumed they probably did, knowing Stefan wouldn't have entrusted me to savage werewolves that bite anything they see and spread their werewolf ways through their bite.

Some thirty minutes or more after leaving the city, and when Toa had just started on the water element, the cars all turned into a pull-out, with the woods reaching out to us in the darkness.

"Everybody out," Tim said, hopping out of the car and opening the door for me. I passed under his intent eyes, his watchfulness calm but detailed, disconcertingly so as he seemed to catch my every movement.

"Why did we stop?" a rough voice demanded, suspicion evident.

Jonas appeared at our side, huge and bulky, causing me a distinct urge to flee. As if he sensed it, Tim took one flowing step, positioning his body between me and Jonas's bulk.

"We go on foot from here," Tim said evenly. "Per Dominicous's instructions, we're taking her to an outpost where she has ample space to learn her craft."

"That's not the plan. You're to take her to the main encampment to learn your way of life."

"Plans change. She'll have plenty of ability to learn where she's going. Plus, defense is easier from that location. I've been told your crew isn't as loyal as some are led to believe…" It was a dig, and appeared to be aimed at Jonas directly. To make his point, Tim stared up at Jonas, the Shape Changer appearing larger than his six feet, the weight in his gaze enough to send an entire army marching.

Jonas bristled, his whole body flexing, readying for action. I stepped back, the car stopping my exit.

"Whoa, whoa!" Charles jumped in, his body the same size as Jonas's, but his movements more like a puppy than a panther. "Jonas, bro, let it go. The Boss approved this. I was there. We're good, bro, we're good."

Jonas stared down at Tim. Tim stared right back, ready. Five people, all about Tim's build, took a step closer, ready to back up their alpha should he need it.

"Now, earth is an interesting element," Toa rattled off, carrying on as if World War III wasn't two seconds away. "It is often the hardest for a person to work, even though it is the most plentiful at any given time. You, I believe, are one of the individuals that suffer from this…"

Jonas's focus switched to the nearly white head of Toa, deep in contemplation. When Jonas looked back at Tim, his eyes showed resignation even if his face showed the love of violence. He didn't nod, step back, or even marginally drop his shoulders, but suddenly the air loosened. The danger had passed. For now.

I was the only one that took a giant breath.

"You two," Tim ordered, addressing his own men at arms. "Stay with Sasha. Now let's go!"

*****

Andris entered Trek's work room at a fast walk. "White Mage, I've got information."

Trek paused with his hands high in the air, the crackle of magic tingling Andris's skin.

"The Council is trying to join with the *Mata*." Andris waited for that information to sink in.

"That was our idea," Trek said in a whine.

Andris had to restrain himself from taking two quick steps and knocking the young fool on the side of the head. He didn't feel like a magical duel today.

In a patient voice a teacher might use, Andris said, "It was, yes. But given that we are just one of a large magical community, and given that the *Mata* are organized, with excellent fighting capabilities, it is logical the Council would seek to make amends."

"But I thought you said that stupid Boss of theirs hates the Shape Changers."

"He does, yes, but he is a company man, and this has come down from the top."

Trek dropped his hands and made his way to a large chair, not quite the throne from his bedroom, but close. He sat with a *plop* and picked at his nail. "What should we do, then?"

"I'm working with another pack up north. They have tie-ins everywhere; people that are loyal to the cause. For now, though, the *Mata* has our girl."

Trek sat up straighter. "Get her!"

"They took her to a remote location, intending to keep it secret. Obviously I had men following their progress to keep an eye on things. I would imagine Stefan would, as well, with how much he trusts the Shape Changers. As soon as we make a move, he'll be alerted."

Andris crossed the room to lean against the wall. "Their position is easy to defend, and they have a large task force of people protecting her; all *Mata.* There are only a couple of our kind, but one is a white mage with power levels above yours. We need to plan this out."

"Above mine?" Trek stared at Andris for a second, his brain churning. "Impossible."

Andris's nostrils flared in irritation. "There are a great many with power that rivals, or exceeds, yours. With a lot more experience."

Trek's eyes widened before his face closed down in indignation. His chin rose, as he apparently chose to ignore that comment. "Can your elusive source sneak her out?"

"Yes. But unless we have a distraction, someone is bound to notice the human's absence. I want her halfway to Canada before Stefan is told she is gone. And we'll need to deal with that link between them."

"And the loyalty of these *Mata*? Will they come over to our way of thinking?"

Andris shook his head, not sure where this was going. "I doubt it. Tim, their alpha, takes great pains to lead normal lives within the human society. He's set some things up that have money rolling in. His people are prospering and happy. He's not going to jeopardize that."

Trek stared at him. "Then they're not needed."

"True…"

"So kill them. There's your distraction. I'll take care of the other mage. Get your source to ferret out the girl. Do you know this *secret*," Trek used his fingers like rabbit ears, "location?"

"Yes. The source is in place."

Trek hopped off the chair. "Good. Plan it. I'll get an army of *Dulcha* at the ready. I'll need some sacrifices, obviously."

"Of course."

Andris left the room strangely hopeful. Trek was a dippy youth, but put a target in front of him, and he busted his ass to claim it. They'd have this girl within the month.

Now, to plan that distraction.

*****

"So… just drape it on?" I asked uncertainly, eyeing the five men and women sitting patiently around the room, allowing themselves to be my guinea pigs. These people had courage in droves—they'd seen some failed spells and still volunteered to help.

We were in the cabin I used as my home base, the middle bunker—as Tim called it—within the cluster of cabins in this remote location. I'd met every one of the shape changers over the last week, a bunch of serious-eyed, combat-ready fighters that went about their duties to secure the location while still making it feel like a home in the woods.

I was in my usual strange situation with them as I had been with everyone else my whole life. Pretty much, regardless of the group of people I found myself with, I was the oddball. At least I was used to it.

Toa stood off to my right, staring. Nothing new there. Jonas, the leader in not trusting the *Mata* for any reason, at any time, sat near the door. He rarely let me out of his sight. Pretty much if I wasn't on the toilet, he was in the same room. And that was only because I threw a tantrum when he tried to linger in the bathroom. Charles was off scouting, making sure Tim was doing a thorough job—Jonas had sent him. And here I was, trying to figure out this magic stuff.

I sighed a lot these days.

"This is not a new spell," Toa said quietly. The man was under the impression I had bionic hearing.

"Yes, but this is the first time I'm trying to do it. Last time it just happened."

"Do it," Jonas barked.

"Oh, yeah, being an impatient a-hole is the right way to help," I muttered.

"We trust you," a slight girl with large, luminous brown eyes said. She, like the other four around her, changed into wolves. They apparently worked together like a wolf pack in the wild, and had been largely assigned to guard me.

Tim didn't trust Stefan's people any more than Jonas trusted the *Mata*. The partnership wouldn't be formed quickly, despite Dominicous's hope.

I called the elements, struggling and working to get and keep control of the tide that threatened to overwhelm me constantly. I shot past the red power level, flew past the orange and gold, slowed down at the white, and landed in black. Toa said I shouldn't practice in anything but the black from now on. That to learn, I had to grow accustomed to my correct magic level. I had to admit, it did make things easier in the spell department.

"Everyone get comfortable," Toa said softly.

Weaving the spell, I let loose and coated the room like a blanket. As the spell sank in, the tiny movements everyone but Toa made ceased. I'd frozen everyone in place.

"I was trying for a light one—you know, so you could still move instead of being totally frozen..." All eyes stared at me, patient. Except for Jonas, who was mad as usual. No mouths moved.

"Right. You guys can't talk. Umm. Okay. I'll try the disintegrate thing." Alarm slowly crept into a few peepers. Like me, they also hoped I didn't blow them up...

I analyzed the spell as movement caught my eye. Like a person walking at full speed toward a freshly cleaned sliding glass door, I knew what would happen a second before it did. Tim's features went *splat* against the clear air-wall of my spell, his limbs hitting a second later. He bounced back, the look of supreme confusion on his face as he stared at nothing in the doorway.

His gaze hit mine as I started to giggle. "It's a thickening spell. Air's solid in here."

"Then why can you move?" He glanced around, smirking when his gaze caught the side of Jonas's motionless face.

"I have no idea, Tim. But as soon as Toa can talk, I'm sure he'll lecture me on that."

"Mhmm," Toa answered.

I gave Tim a *see?* look.

Tim glanced at Jonas again and let a small smile quirk the lips. He looked back at me. "Can I talk to you for a moment?" Tim motioned me out of the room.

Tim was trying to irritate Jonas, which I could definitely get behind. I glanced around the patient faces. "I should probably try to get them out of this."

"It'll only take a moment."

"Mmm mmm," Jonas hummed, trying to prevent my leaving with a wordless growl.

Jonas still wasn't my favorite person, what with trying to get me killed and all. And being that no one else liked him, either, I figured they'd be okay with hanging out for a minute while I pissed him off. "Sure."

Outside the room, Tim leaned against the wall, surveying me. "I wanted to check in with you. Make sure you had everything you needed."

I bobbed my head. "I do, thanks! Everyone is being really nice and helpful."

"And the crew that came with you? Is Jonas treating you okay?" Steel crept into his voice, his bearing relaxed but the edge in his words hinting he could turn lethal in the blink of an eye.

"He's being Jonas. Hovering around, shooting everyone angry glares, and making sure I don't step out of line. Stefan sent him, so…" I shrugged. Like Charles, I wondered if sending Jonas was the best idea, but Stefan knew what he was doing. I knew he would do everything in his power to protect me, even if he couldn't be with me. If he thought Jonas would do that, I wouldn't question.

Besides, there was a huge camp of mean, fighting, potentially furry bodyguards. I'd be fine.

Tim, probably thinking the same thing, said, "Okay. Well, let me know if you need anything. Or if you have any questions.

Everyone says you're really trying to learn our ways and fit in, so I want to help you as much as possible with that. Ignorance is dividing us from Stefan's crew—I want to combat that any way I can."

I smiled at him, because it was a really sweet thing to say. Anyone that could help me fit in was A-Okay in my book. "I better try to unravel that spell. Or charm. I still don't know the difference."

"Why don't you ask Toa?" Tim walked me back to the room. "He seems to have a well of knowledge."

"I did. And he explained it. But he's so hard to focus on. I find myself nodding off after the first thirty seconds."

Tim laughed and watched me reenter the room. He continued to watch, probably in fascination, as I frowned at the air and busted my brain trying to figure out how to unravel the spell. After a while of pawing at nothingness, I found the hairline cracks in my spell, and began pulling apart the fibers little by little. Carefully.

Finally, my face drenched with sweat, I plucked the last magical knot and felt the spell disintegrate into nothing.

"Much better," Toa said, stepping forward as if he hadn't been frozen for the last fifteen minutes.

"Don't step out of here when I'm immobile," Jonas commanded.

I rolled my eyes, then immediately lost focus as Toa started to explain about that spell and how it worked.

A few hours later and I found myself traipsing through the bare halls of the main cabin. Fierce-eyed men and women, gliding with a killer's grace not unlike Stefan's clan, passed on their way to their duties, or maybe just after eating and heading to settle in somewhere and relax.

While the *Mata* weren't night creatures, they didn't seem to keep normal hours, either. It seemed like they prowled half the night, slept way late, and started their day near noon. Basically, it was like living with a bunch of bartenders. Being that I got to see the sunlight with that schedule, while still keeping Toa happy, it was the schedule everyone kept.

Jonas grumbled about it constantly.

"Mage." A stocky shape changer titled his head at me in greeting as he passed.

He just called me mage! I couldn't help the foolish grin as I sauntered into the large kitchen and dining area. I had no idea why Jonas and Stefan hated these people—they seemed really cool to me.

Three burly men sat at the far end of a large wood table, hunched over their plates with wide smiles. As I entered, their eyes flicked my way. Their bodies straightened up marginally, smiles dwindling. Each gave me a nod hello.

"You guys don't need to act all serious around me. You're not on duty or anything," I mumbled, turning right, toward the worn lime green kitchen island. Unlike Stefan's mansion, which was kept pristine and refined, these cabins were mostly older and worked in. Clean, but not current. Did the same job, though.

"Don't mind them," a pixie-like girl with a shock of bright blue hair said as she strolled in. She scooped a mound of mashed potatoes out of the bowl on the island and dumped it onto her plate. "They think the sun shines out of their asses."

Without turning around, the men at the table facing us straightened even more. Huge shoulders rolled. "We *know* the sun shines out of our asses, actually, "the one in the middle said, "and if you'd care to put your money where your mouth is, I'd show you."

"No, thanks. I don't like seeing hairy full moons." The girl winked at me with a smirk. The other two guys at the table huffed out a laugh. One slapped the butt of the joke on the back with a hearty guffaw.

"Hilarious," he drawled, standing up with his plate in his hands. He flashed the blue-haired girl a glare as he stalked our way.

Magic filled me instantly. I wasn't sure what this guy would do, but was ready to unleash hell if he got violent.

The man gave me a wide berth as he entered the kitchen area, but veered in close to the blue-haired girl. Lightning-quick he reached toward her, his plate still in his free hand.

A blast of electricity zipped through me as I feared he might strike her. Pure black shot out of my hands, wrapping around his body and squeezing.

"What the *fu—?"* The word ended in a wheeze.

"What's happening?" one of the other guys barked, jumping up from the table. The wooden table surface jolted, knocking the remaining two plates to the ground. They crashed to the floor, food and porcelain splashing across linoleum.

"Don't kill him, Sasha," the girl said, a grin spreading up her face as she watched the man turn purple. "He was just trying to make me flinch. Haven't been paying attention to the magical woman you were sent here to guard, have you, Rodge? Didn't realize she acts first and thinks later when someone she knows is in danger. Not so detailed in your job, hmmm?"

Rodge wheezed harder as I worked on unraveling the spell.

"Sorry—I thought you were going to hit her," I squeaked.

"What'd she do?" one of the rescue party asked, standing just where the linoleum of the dining room changed into tile of the kitchen.

The spell peeled away. Rodge took a huge, lung-filling breath, leaning forward against the island.

"She got him with a spell, obviously." The girl speared a piece of roast beef with a fork and hauled it onto her plate. "You guys better clean up that mess before the Alpha comes in here."

Rodge shot me a glare. With wooden movements, he dropped his plate, miraculously unscathed, into the dishwasher.

As he moved away, leaving his two comrades to clean up their mess, the girl titled her head toward the food spread out on the counter. "Help yourself. I'm Ann, by the way. The one with the mullet over there is Pete."

The guy on his hands and knees, wiping up spilled food, glanced up. "It's not a mullet. I just haven't had time to get to the barber."

"Uh huh. And the other one is John."

A man with bushy eyebrows and a receding hairline said, "Hi." He jerked his head toward Pete. "It is a mullet, isn't it?"

Pete straightened up with a pained expression. "The back just grows faster than the sides. I can't help if that every time I *change* my hair gets a weird urge to Rapunzel down my back."

"Anyway, don't worry about Rodge," Ann continued, laughing. "Being a shape changer goes right to his head. Thinks he's invincible or something. Isn't that right, guys? You all think you're God's gift."

John huffed, a smile tweaking his lips. "You're one to talk. Wasn't it you that challenged the Alpha right after you changed?"

Ann's face went crimson, but she smiled at me. "I totally did. I just felt so...*strong!* How about you? Do you get stronger with the magic?"

The guys paused, staring at me.

Still tingly from the scene a couple moments ago, and a little shocked that Rodge didn't try to throw me through a window, I carefully picked up a plate with a shaking hand. "No, I didn't get any stronger. And, as you apparently know, I don't really have a firm control over my magic."

Ann waved my comment away as she headed toward the table. Pete said, "It took me a few years to have a firm grip on changing. You can't just learn everything right away. It takes a while. You have that vampire-looking-dude to help you out, though, right?"

I giggled. I couldn't help myself. "He does look like a vampire, doesn't he?"

"I thought the myths were true when I first saw him," Ann admitted, cutting her meat. "What's with the staring?"

"I *know,* right?" I laughed as I moved toward the table with my plate. "Drives me crazy. But he knows what he's doing."

Pete leaned against the door frame. "Always helps to have a good teacher. Listen to that guy and you'll have all this down lickety-split. Well, nice to meet you, Sasha. See ya later."

"See ya." John gave a salute as he followed Pete out the room.

"They're friendly," I said before I shoveled some mashed potatoes into my mouth. Constantly working with magic, and the energy drain that went with it, had me famished.

"Yeah, everyone here is pretty cool. We're family. Changing for the first time is really scary. It hurts, it's foreign, you turn into a thing out of story books, and you think you're going to die. I freaked out for the first year. Didn't ever want to change. Tim coached me through it."

"He's a good leader, then?"

Ann nodded adamantly. "He's the backbone of this whole outfit. That guy bleeds for the pack. He'd do anything for any one of us. A lot of us would be running around wild, terrified and getting dead if he didn't create the structure we have now. Yeah, it's good here. I'm used to what I am, now, but at first..." She shook her head. "It was a hard first year."

I took a steadying breath. "I'm still in that first year."

Ann leaned against the table, surveying me. "You don't really fit in, huh? I mean, you're human, so that's gotta be weird, right? Hanging out with a bunch of giant dudes with perpetual boners..."

I choked out a laugh, spraying food. I raked the back of my hand across my face. "Don't do that when I'm eating!"

She chuckled and cut off a bit of her meat. "What? Spread my hilariousness around?"

"Yes, exactly." I sobered. "And yes, it's a little…lonely. Where I'm at."

She beamed. "Was lonely. We aren't exactly the same, I guess, but we both started out human, and we both had to get used to what we've become, right? So, now you got a partner in crime. Which is great, because I have a great idea for a practical joke, and I can't think of anyone that would hate it more than that surly bodyguard of yours."

Excited laughter bubbled out of my chest. "I'm in."

"Where is he by the way?" Ann glanced at the door.

"I gave him the slip. He'll be around soon. He's pretty good at tracking me down, unfortunately."

The large form of Jonas appearing in the doorway punctuated my words. I really missed privacy.

*****

"So this is what it's come to?" Jonas asked a few days into their protection detail as he watched Sasha. She stood in the clearing beyond the cabins with Toa, working at some spell or other. "This is what more than a decade of good service gets you? Watching some human pet play at magic? The borders are open, our enemy is pushing at us, making a bunch of noise, and here we are, sitting on our asses, staring at some dumb human?"

"How do you know what's happening with the borders?" Charles asked more lightly than he felt like asking.

"Unlike you, I keep tabs on my surroundings. I'm not going to let the Boss take us all down because he's infatuated."

"Unlike *you,"* Charles returned with an edge to his voice, "I trust the Boss's judgment. She's at black power level, Jonas. *Black.* That's the highest you can reach. Protecting her from getting snatched is ten times more important than chasing some purple *Dulcha* back across our border. Plus, half the time, she summons up all sorts of crap that keeps us on our toes. Maybe you should drop the pity party and be a team player for once. Or do you have interests outside of our clan…?"

Jonas swung his gaze away from a flailing Toa enshrouded in black smoke.

Charles felt his skin prickle within Jonas's hostile glare, as if he stared into the eyes of a predator, the gaze flat and unwavering. "Be careful, Boy Wonder. You might be the Boss's favorite now, but when he gets tired of the human, you won't be much more than a baby with a Watch Command badge again."

Charles shook his head, forcing himself to look away. Human males stalked the perimeter of the clearing, using all their senses to guard. If Charles was honest with himself, besides the fact that these *Mata* changed into animals, they had a lot of the same characteristics his kind did. Their vision wasn't much improved, but their hearing, their smell, and their prowess would top a normal human any day. Plus, they had this extra sense. Somehow magical, they could perceive things.

Charles had no idea how that perceiving thing worked. He could walk up to one of the shifters, absolutely silent, and he or she'd turn around and notice him as if he'd been as loud as Sasha. At breakfast earlier that morning, he'd basically tiptoed in. He'd made sure his clothes didn't even make a rustle. But sure enough, a really hot chick with her back to him had asked if he wanted coffee when he was only a couple steps into the room!

How did she know? It was a little creepy.

He didn't want to ask about it, though. The *Mata* didn't seem to like his kind much. And of course the Boss and everyone older than Charles hated the *Mata*, so there was that. No one talked about it, but there was history.

"She can't even do magic correctly," Jonas growled, bringing Charles out of his reflections.

"She's new to it. She wasn't raised with it," Charles shot back. He noticed a man at the edge of the clearing bracing, readying for a fight. A second later he was stripping out of his clothes.

Sasha paused in her ministrations, halting Toa with her. They looked toward the tree line. Charles stood as the male's body blurred strangely, a blast of magic flaring. Skin morphed into fur, creating a huge wolf larger and broader than a Great Dane. Fighting one of them, with the teeth and claws and all that, would be…uncomfortable.

"Cool!" Sasha exclaimed.

A second later, Charles was running at the daft idiot. Toa, thinking just as fast, wrapped himself and Sasha in a white bubble, making a shield. At least one of them had sense. As Jonas joined Charles around the two mages, the rest of the clearing filled with wolves, ten in all, working together in defense like a wolf pack would.

Three members of Charles's clan stepped into the clearing; Adnan, Mira, and, "Oh great," Charles muttered. Darla. They traveled with a member of Tim's pack, a male that changed into a Tiger, fierce and nasty when pushed to it. Jonas tried to push him to it, often.

Strangely, Toa kept the shield and the wolves kept their lupine form, teeth bared, surrounding the newcomers. Charles and Jonas stepped forward.

"Why are you here?" Jonas asked, his attention focused on Adnan. "Aren't you supposed to be in class or something? This ain't a daycare."

Adnan raised his chin but didn't have time to answer before Darla waved the thought away. "The Boss suspects a leak. We've come to warn you and provide a few more bodies . I'm also here to ensure the human is getting a proper magical education." She eyed Toa with disdain.

"Stefan sent *you?"* Sasha blurted, hands at her hips.

Darla stared down at the human with her beautiful face perfectly flat. "I am still in line for the mate title, *human.* He might have a sophomoric interest in you now, but he is a business man. He wants all his future assets in one place. If you don't work out, who do you think will take the mate title? And if something happens to me, there is Mira."

Sasha visibly deflated as Toa nodded. The white shield winked out. "Let us get back to it," Toa stated as he eyed Darla. "You may watch, but you may not interfere. If you have a problem with the way I am going about things, you are free to scurry back to your liege and tell on me, as you see fit."

Darla's eyes smoldered as she stared at the blond creep, receiving that strange blue-eyed gaze in return. She flicked her beautiful head and huffed. Toa turned to Sasha.

"Commence."

"In front of *her?"* Sasha asked in a small voice.

Charles's heart went out to her, but the Boss was doing the right thing. If Sasha couldn't pull this off, he needed a mate, and Darla was the best contender. Still sucked for poor Sasha, though. She didn't need the reminder that she was human, and might not be good enough.

Chapter 7

"I did it!" Sasha's glance flew around the living room in the main cabin, landing on Charles. He momentarily dropped his knitting. "Charles, look. The dog-thing found me without shocking me. Finally. It only took the better part of a freaking week."

A black, smoky blob fizzled at her feet. The intent had been to leave a charm in a place an enemy might travel. Then, when said enemy stepped through, the magic would return-to-sender with a light hum, alerting of trespassers. In the past Sasha had always gotten one hell of a shock. Today, she'd done it. She was making strides.

They sat in the living area of the largest log cabin, Toa wanting to be indoors to reduce the amount of distraction for Sasha. Jonas stood by the door, looking into the hall, monitoring someone's progress toward the room. Either that, or looking at the ghost that set off that charm. Charles, as usual, sat in a chair, ready to have magic blasted at him at a moment's notice. While Sasha was getting a hundred times better, she still had mishaps. None so far tonight, but Charles knew better than to get his hopes up.

"Good." Toa glided over to her in that creepy way he had. "That is a moderate charm which those with less than red power levels cannot achieve. Now we will take the next step up."

Moderate? Charles was suddenly extremely glad he was both violent, and great with a sword, because no way could he do that spell with any sort of results. He had plenty of power, but he'd never been great at magical finesse.

Sasha took a big breath as Toa started explaining something to do with the elements fire and water. The man could bore a plant with the way he droned on. Judging by Sasha's quickly glazing eyes, her mind was already drifting.

"I shall demonstrate," Toa cut off suddenly. Sasha wasn't the only one learning.

Pure white magic drifted into existence, creating a beach ball sized orb in the center of the room. Translucent, it hovered beautifully, reminding Charles of the first snowfall of winter.

"Now, walk into it," Toa instructed Sasha.

"No." Jonas straightened, stepping further into the room. "That spell can kill."

"By applying the proper defensive magic, and if the sphere is a solid color, then yes, it will kill if the caster has enough power. This sphere, as you can see, is not solid. It will simply be unpleasant," Toa explained patiently.

"Oh, fantastic," Sasha muttered.

"Ah, yes, baby steps," Darla said in a silky purr as she stepped into the room behind Jonas.

"What're you doing here?" Jonas asked in a thick growl.

"Assessing the level of training. Making sure our star pupil is worth all of our time. The sooner she fails, the sooner I'll be back on top." Darla gracefully lowered herself into a chair beside the door, her legs peeking out from the slit in her shimmery dress all the way to her enticing upper thigh.

Charles's mouth went dry. He hadn't had sex in a while. Those damn *Mata* were worse than Sasha for being prudes. Well, not worse, but certainly as bad. And more violent, too. He'd merely *hinted* to one of their females that he was available should she need a ride. He did not appreciate the sudden punch to the balls. It had been completely uncalled for. A simple 'no thanks' would've done the trick.

Charles huffed with the memory as Toa turned. As if on a hinge, his shoulders swiveled, sparing one glance for the new arrival. She gave him a scorching glance and licked her lips, probably desperate for a drop of his blood. Toa turned back to Sasha just as slowly, somehow failing to get wood. Unlike Charles.

"Walk through the sphere please, so you can try it." Toa elegantly gestured Sasha toward the floating ball. "You only seem to learn when you experience something. I am simply instructing in the approach that is most likely to be received."

"Okay, but what's the point of it?" Sasha asked dubiously, stalling. "You can see it. Why would someone just walk into a magical ball? I think I'd avoid it."

"In battle, you can create one of these and send it floating. If you have sufficient energy, you can take down a few unaware or distracted fighters." Toa gestured her forward.

Sasha's eyes flicked to Darla's chair. The other woman winked, her smile smug. Taking a determined breath, Sasha stepped forward slowly. As her face and torso drifted into the bubble, she gave a huge jolt.

"Holy—□

She stepped back quickly, rubbing her arms. "Dang it, Toa. That hurt!"

"Yes, it is not pleasant. Now you try."

Charles suddenly did not want to be in this room. If she managed to do the spell, he'd have to test it because Jonas ranked higher than him in the violence department. If Toa's spell hurt, hers would probably blast his face off.

For all the work Jonas did with this detail, it was a wonder he'd come with them at all. Charles had no idea what the Boss was thinking on that score. Jonas hated Sasha, didn't want to be here, but wouldn't let her out of his sight, thus being a hostile nuisance to everyone else. Plus, he didn't help with any of the unpleasant stuff. If he wasn't so damn hostile and wound up, Charles would have mentioned it.

They all needed to get laid. That was one of the problems right there.

"Okay," Sasha said as the white sphere melted back into the air. Her brow creased.

"Show me, please," Toa instructed in his sing-song voice.

Sasha put up her hand, palm toward the ceiling. A colored wisp drifted above her skin, deep red. Now orange. Quickly to gold.

"Slower, please," Toa said.

Sasha's lips parted, her breath falling out of her open mouth heavily. Her other hand clenched at her side as the wisp eased past burnished gold and into white. She was trying to slow the draw, but based on her rigid body, having a hard time of it. Finally, the wisp was a deep, bottomless pit of black, sucking in the light around it. Full power.

"Good. Now..." Toa gave her a sweeping hand gesture.

Jonas stepped out through the doorway, an orange shield blocking Sasha's magic. Toa flicked up a white shield as red wrapped around Darla. Charles was last, nearly having forgotten to raise his shield. If the Boss trusted Jonas, there was no reason Charles shouldn't. Especially in the face of whatever was coming.

"Okay," Sasha said again, her brows dipping down her nose in concentration. "I'm trying to create a moving sphere to sideswipe people who aren't paying attention. I'm aiming for pain, not death. Okay..."

She put her hands up, palms facing each other. Blackness materialized in front of her like pixilated smoke. Her brow started to glisten as she concentrated, her fingers trembling. The black took shape, ball-like, though too dense. Then denser.

"Not so much," Toa warned in a gentle voice.

Charles started to cringe.

Perfectly round now, outsides glistening like it was coated in oil. Charles's skin started to tingle furiously, magic crackling the air. The ball started to wobble, losing shape but not density.

"I'm losing it," Sasha said through clenched teeth.

Toa stepped forward. White frost enveloped the black, freezing the oil slick. Another moment had the outside cracking like ice, both Toa and Sasha now battling with flexed bodies and grim faces. In a whoosh, magic flooded the room, pounding against Charles's shield, threatening to erode it away. Darla shrieked as her red was sandblasted, her hands in front of her face in a defense posture, pain lacing her expression.

In another second it was all over, Sasha and Toa left panting in the middle of the room, Darla with a crazy mask of rage.

"*This* is what you've learned?" Darla spat, standing up with a red face. "You've been here for two weeks! You've been in classes for weeks before that, and *this* is all you can do? You can't even control your magic, let alone contain it. You're dangerous, human. No wonder the Boss sent me. There's no way you can lead our people. You can't even look after yourself!"

"She is working with more than twice the flow you are," Toa said calmly, completely unruffled by her tirade. "You could not possibly understand the effects of drawing that much power, since you reside in meager red. I will only say that it is slippery and dangerous, and you will never experience it no matter how much, or whose blood you take. You, simply, don't have the ability to hold it. Now, Sasha, let's chat about what went wrong as we ready for bed."

Sasha's gaze had fallen, now focused on the floor in front of her feet. She stuffed her hands in her pockets, following behind Toa like a kicked puppy. She didn't raise her eyes in defiance as she passed Darla and out the door. Toa might not have been worried about Sasha's lack of material progress, but Sasha clearly was.

Charles wished he knew what to say to her. She would learn control of her magic, Charles was certain—that girl rose to the occasion when she had to. But she wouldn't believe him if he told her that.

That bitch Darla didn't help matters by throwing it in her face, either.

As Sasha disappeared, Jonas stepped to the door to follow, having entered the room again after the magic was diminished.

"You got it, bro?" Charles asked as he dropped his knitting into the basket beside his chair. "I might get a quick workout before I tuck into bed. I didn't get to kill any of Sasha's creations today."

Jonas spared him a glance before nodding. When he turned back, he ran smack into Darla.

"Running away so soon? I thought maybe we could—□

Jonas's hand came up…and *wiped* Darla away as if she was a curtain covering the doorway. Limbs flailing, she went staggering out of the way, Jonas already strolling out. Charles couldn't help laughing.

"What is his problem these days?" Darla muttered as she straightened herself out. Her heat-soaked eyes hit Charles, now the only one in the room, almost as an afterthought. She paused for a moment, and then her body seemed to lose all its bones and kinda slink down into a shrine of sex.

Oh, no.

Charles tried to stand in a hurry, but his hard-on got painful when her dress gave in to gravity and shimmered down her nude body. Perfectly round breasts stared him in the face. This was the absolute *worst* time to be sex starved.

"You'll do," she purred with a sultry smile, crossing the room.

"No, no—I have stuff to do. And I don't like giving blood. I'll just…"

Her tinkling laugh filled up the room as she stopped right in front of him. Her knee bent forward and nudged his legs wider apart. She stepped closer, his legs pushed out to accommodate her body. She bent low, her breasts passing by his vision as her beautiful face leveled with his. Her tongue slipped across his bottom lip.

"Feel how wet I am, Charles."

She raised her leg and braced it to the side of his groin, just barely putting pressure on his pounding dick. Her hand grabbed his and directed it to the middle of her thighs, the tips of his fingers brushing her wet slit.

The pounding got ten times harder to ignore.

A breast graced his lips, its budded nipple nudging. "C'mon, Charles, I won't bite if you really don't want me to."

He rubbed deeper, working the wetness, not needing guidance anymore. His tongued her taut nipple, causing a low moan from Darla. She was crazy, and vindictive, and unpredictable, and would definitely bite him if he stopped paying attention, but…

"What's a little sex among friends?" Charles muttered, opening his mouth and sucking in her breast. Two fingers worked into her, feeling along the inner wall, as she pushed into him with a groan.

"I underestimated you. You know *exactly* what you're doing," Darla breathed, pumping her hips into his hand.

She leaned back, popping her breast out of his mouth. Grinding into his hand now, she fed him the other breast, her hips swooping into him expertly. He wasn't the only one that knew what he was doing. She might give him a run for his money.

But he'd rise to the occasion like a champ.

He massaged with his thumb as his fingers plunged, working the suction at her nipple just right. Her breathing started to get labored and her movements more frantic. She clutched his hair in two fistfuls and yanked, screaming while she orgasmed in giant body spasms.

"Oh, *yes,* Charles!" Darla slowed and languidly took her knee off of his leg.

She smiled down on him. "My turn."

Her hair swished over her shoulders as she bent, her deft fingers working the fly of his jeans. Cool air assaulted his erection, giving him the best kind of shivers. Before he could acclimate, her hot hand had his shaft and she was running her palm against him firmly.

"Nice and big. My kinda toy." Her body bent further as she knelt between his legs. A warm, wet tongue licked up his sack before she sucked it in.

"Oh!" Charles didn't know whether to push forward, or fall back with his eyes rolled back in his head. He didn't have to worry about it. The next second had her tongue licking up the back of his shaft and tickling along his crease, just about to take it all…

"Ohh, shit." He leaned back, his eyes rolling back. Her hot mouth sucked his brain out of his dick, reaching through his body and wiping out all his thoughts. Not that he had many to begin with. He felt his tip reach deep down, all the way to the back of her throat, as her chin met his ends.

Maybe he wouldn't rise like a champ. This female made him feel like a novice.

Charles held onto the chair with all his might as he watched his erection pump in and out of her mouth. He could barely stand it. He was already close.

Reading his situation, she straightened up suddenly and draped a long leg over his lap. With her hand, she took his shaft in a firm grip and worked his tip along her slit. His shaking hands gripped her hips as she sat down with all her weight.

"Oh, gods. Oh, holy gods. Holy moly." Then speech ran out as she bounced on top of him, her breasts jiggling in his face merrily, her sex stroking his.

His balls tightened up and his stomach clenched. His whole body compressed, magic leaking out.

"That's right," she purred, gyrating over him now, leaning those glorious breasts against his chest. "Fall into it."

The friction got more intense. She reached between them and ripped at his shirt, tearing it down the middle. Her taut nipples rubbed his skin. Her hot breath soaked into his neck.

So close now. Just about...

He felt the pinch right before one glorious, deep pull through the center of this body.

"N*ooooooooohh!*"

He shook her off his neck as his body erupted, exploding into her. He shuddered so hard he might've been sitting on a fault line in an earthquake.

"Oh, gods," he said, panting. He pushed her away again as her lips aimed for his neck.

"No biting." He leaned back against the chair, holding her shoulders. "Against the rules."

He barely registered her pout. "You're not done yet, are you?"

He groaned. "You want more?"

"Of course. I hear you've got great stamina."

This was the first time in history he hated that rumor.

Her mouth licked down his bare chest, her tongue circling a nipple. Her hand started working him again, light and tickling. Playful. Expert.

Just as he was reviving, putting his all into the recovery, he felt another pinch. Like a tug through his pec, down through his stomach, and pulling on the inside of his balls, his dick became a live wire, deep and intimate. And she was the last female he wanted to share this kind of intimacy with.

"No, no—no blood. I'll stop right now, I swear to the gods I will." Charles pushed her face away again, a dribble of blood dripping down his chest.

With a smile, she licked at it before continuing down. And down. Her mouth took in his almost hardness, sucking so hard he yelped.

"Hang in there, it'll be worth it." She winked at him.

He wasn't so sure anymore.

Another swallow, sucking hard and deep. He butted the end of her throat. Completely hard now and in his stride. He palmed her head and helped push her down, grinding in there good and deep. She took to it in greedy gulps like a pro.

Before he had to tell her he was nearly there again—so he didn't have to start from scratch with the hard-on, because that might kill him—she pulled off, his erection bobbing in the air. Moving quick, not losing momentum, she sucked at his balls. Very nice.

The pinch was in his inner thigh this time.

"Damn it, woman. You're like a piranha." He jerked away.

With an evil smile, she crawled back into his lap.

"Last time, though. I need to hit the sack," Charles warned, dropping his finger to the top of her slit to make sure she got where she needed to go. He wouldn't admit it out loud, but she was a bit above his caliber. The Boss was a real man to deal with this all the time.

Facing him, she clutched his shaft again, this time directing it to the opening in the back. Slowly she sat, his tip working into that tight hole.

"Oh, my…oh. You're into that, huh? *Oh!*"

He couldn't focus. That hole was so deep and tight. So hot. Lips nibbled at his neck. His finger worked her nub. That glorious friction had his dick tingling already, needing to orgasm so hard all he heard was white noise.

And then the pinch came again on his neck.

The pull sucked through his whole body, sweet and deep and so-fucking-good. He couldn't back her off this time. Not with that deliciously tight hole. And the friction. And the blessed pull.

"Oh, holy gods," Charles moaned, lightheaded and delirious. He pumped into her, that suction on his neck pushing him higher, her ass muscles clutching him like a fist.

Warning bells went off, but he couldn't focus. Or function. All he could do was close his eyes and pump like an animal. Beyond reason. His balls screamed to let go. His body flexed. His fingers dug into her hips.

Blessed release. Hard and fast. He slammed into her, groaning in ecstasy. Unable to help calling her name in bliss.

His head lolled, his body totally spent. She backed off his neck.

"Thanks, pet. Your blood hit just the spot." She wiped her face with a smirk. As she left, she swooped down and snatched her dress off the ground.

He hated her laugh as she left the room.

Well. That happened. He'd given a nasty bitch a bunch of blood. Fantastic.

He swore at himself as he stood, swaying slightly as his body registered the amount of blood she'd stolen. He walked across the grounds with his dick dangling. No sense in trying for decorum now—he'd given up his pride to the top of the sexual food chain. So much for no means no.

He kind of felt like one of those human chicks in the movies after she got used like a tool. Kind of manhood stripping, he'd say that much.

He entered the cabin he shared with Sasha and Jonas. As he walked down the hall to his room, knowing there was no way he was working out right now, Sasha stepped out of the bathroom. Her eyes did a quick assessment before her face fell.

"You didn't."

"Don't want to talk about it."

"With *her,* though, Charles? She sucks."

Charles stripped off his shirt and threw it in a ball into the bathroom. "I know this. I was outgunned."

Sasha's eyes snagged on the quickly healing cuts on his neck. "You gave her *blood?* Charles, what the hell is wrong with you?"

"He's a young twerp that barely knows how to use his dick." Jonas passed by without a glance. "Lets every species he sees bowl him over. And this is my partner."

"Oh, great, yes. Rub it in, everybody. Even better." Charles wiped spit off his chest. "Can you two just shove off? I need some alone time."

"Is this because I won't do you? Is this spite?"

Charles turned to Sasha, stared at her for one second, and then slammed the door in her face. They just didn't understand. Until you were in the lion's mouth, you had no idea how sharp the teeth were.

He felt like a schmuck.

Chapter 8

The next day, I sat on a plush leather couch in the common room. A few other people within the room cleaned, read, or relaxed, each doing their own thing. A book lay open in my lap, staring at me as I stared back at it. All I saw were black letters on a white page, blending together as my eye focused and unfocused. I couldn't stop thinking about Stefan protecting his interests. I logically knew he had to, and Toa had explained it in depth, but it still stung. It meant he didn't have the utmost faith in me like he said he did. Being that I had never had faith in myself, it left me feeling empty and forlorn.

"It's going to work out, seriously." Ann leaned against the bookcase, supposed to be off doing something, but when she saw me mope into the room, she followed. "Just as soon as you get your head around the magic, you'll wipe the floor with Miss Runway."

"So you say."

"I *do* say. Sasha, listen to me. You need to have a little faith. You need to walk before you sprint, you know? Just--□

"Alpha."

I looked up in time to notice Tim enter the room, his eyes gleaming with that predatory light this group of Shape Changers was known for. The man at the desk came out of a shallow bow, continuing whatever paperwork he had been contemplating. A woman, young and spry, closed her book, stood and offered a slightly deeper bow, her eyes shining with stars, and her face flushing a desire-ridden rose. "Alpha."

Ann's face went bright red, caught somewhere other than at her post. She bobbed her head in jerky movements. *Busted.* "Alpha."

She glanced my way, her eyes riddled with panic. "Gotta go, Sasha. I'll talk to you later, okay?"

"Aren't you supposed to be working the perimeter?" Tim asked, flaying Ann with a hard stare.

"Yes, Alpha. Just headed there now." She very nearly sprinted from the room.

Tim watched her go before stalking through, not offering an acknowledgement of the respectful diffidence of the others in the room. His eyes burned into mine as I tried to rip my gaze away from the power in that stare. I was used to Stefan, however, and if my backbone wouldn't allow me to drop my gaze before his, which was stronger and more forceful than this guy, I certainly wasn't going to drop it for a near stranger.

"Sasha." He seemed to be trying to soften his gravel-infused voice. Apparently thinking I scared easily. Probably not wanting to get hit with an unpredictable blast of magic.

"Hi, Tim," I responded, scooting over so he could sit next to me.

He angled his body toward me, glancing at the book on my lap for a second before honing in on my face. "How goes it?"

"Not well. Toa lectures me about my magic, tells me how to use it, and then expects that to be enough. It just doesn't sink in. So, I try to mimic him, and I blow things up or create monsters. *Then* he yells at me because I'm doing things in opposite land."

I didn't want to admit that Stefan was right to send Darla. That I wasn't getting it; that I was letting him down.

"You need a practical lesson. I had a great many new subjects that had never attempted a controlled change. I needed to work through it with them. Explanations are for theoretical knowledge. They don't help with actually *doing* something."

"I know, but no one has my type of magic. No one can show me."

"Well, keep at it. You'll get it. Stefan seems to have faith in you, so you need to have faith in yourself. That is one of the biggest needs in any type of leadership role. You can't second-guess yourself or wander around without a purpose. If you do, people will think you aren't in control."

"I'm *not* in control. And Stefan has so much faith he sent Darla into harm's way."

"He is a great statistician with risk and a great leader." Tim paused for a moment, and then placed a comforting arm around my shoulders. "I don't know if his actions were right or wrong, but I, too, thought he had more faith than to send reinforcements. Nonetheless, he has his reasons. Maybe the decision isn't what it seems. Maybe he is vying for the Regional position and wants to leave a successor."

"I don't know, but crying about it isn't going to help." I blew out a frustrated breath. "What I really want to do is just punch her in the mouth."

"Atta girl," Tim said softly.

"How come you guys can change into animals?" I asked to sidetrack the conversation.

Tim sat farther back, his arm still around my shoulders, continuing to lend support which I took greedily. "We think it's a mutation in a person's genetic makeup. Unlike Stefan's kind, we are all human. At some point in a person's life, we develop what the doctors think is an advanced stage of cancer. We either get treatment or we get a terminal date. In some people, it takes a few months to make the change, some longer, but the body priming is a painful affair. The person affected stops eating, has to stay in bed, loses sleep—you can see why they continue to think it is cancer even though some medical tests might seem strange. At the end of the body's transformation, the person undergoes their first full change, which is often scary and sometimes dangerous.

"We try to find these potential Shape Changers and help them through the change. We can smell it coming, you see. The body's chemistry changes, changing a person's scent. If we get there in time, we can help a person through it. If not, we have to hope they don't endanger themselves or others. Some have gotten shot because the townspeople thought a wild animal prowled the streets."

"I bet. If I was walking around willy-nilly and saw a giant wolf I'd be a bit nervous, all right."

"Exactly. We are pretty good, though. We constantly have people looking. There aren't so many that make the change."

"But, that's in this area. What about the rest of the world?"

"This…affliction happens all over the world. Like Stefan's kind, we have a larger pack system. We've had to develop it to keep our people under the radar—keep us safe. If potential mutants landed in human hands, we'd spend our lives in a research facility or be hunted."

I nodded, because that was a very realistic view of what scientists would do. And if they didn't, the Homeland Security people would step in, trying to engineer a new weapon. Or just kill on sight.

"Is that why you are joining with Stefan? To unite forces?"

"It's smart. Plus, we were approached by Andris. They are trying to organize a power shift with humans. They want to dominate, and to do that, they need to up their numbers. We were a logical choice, of course. We are human, and exist within the human society. What better group of people to infiltrate, and then bring the humans down from the inside. But in that way lies death, which Stefan and his Council know from experience. Andris is smart, but power hungry. He will eventually emerge from the shadows, but not until he has a clear way. I am trying to help Stefan put up a roadblock."

"I'm supposed to help with that."

"And you will," Tim said softly, his eyes losing their alpha strength. I marveled at their soft depth, their color a deep auburn.

"What animal do you change into?" I asked, entranced by those eyes.

"A Kodiak," he whispered.

I noticed for the first time his face, broad and defined, with a strong jaw and straight nose. He was a handsome man, if no Stefan, with strength and power tempered by a slow way about him. "Are there many grizzlies?"

"No, just one. We have quite a few wolves, a few large cats, some smaller animals; an all-around mix."

"So if you bite me, I won't turn into an animal?" I smiled, hiding the gulp when his eyes traveled my face.

"You will, but only until climax." He chuckled, prompting an edge of uncertainty to crawl into my awareness.

I turned my face away, suddenly hyper-aware of our proximity. "Anyway," I said, "I should probably go and find Charles. He gets in trouble when left to his own devices for too long."

"He said the same thing about you yesterday evening."

I snorted. Figured.

As I stood and headed for the door, my book forgotten, Tim said, "And Sasha…"

I turned back, seeing Tim stand, his large shoulders straining the cotton of his t-shirt, currently molding to his defined pecks like spray paint. "Yeah?"

"Watch out for Jonas, okay? He's made it pretty clear he doesn't trust humans."

The only reminder I needed on that score seemed to come from Jonas himself whenever we were in the same room. That hard stare was not easy to forget. Neither were the warning tingles up my back.

A stocky man with giant arms stepped in front of me as I tried to exit the room, his eyes, a weird shade of light hazel, almost gold, rooted me in place and had my tongue sticking to the roof of my mouth.

"Something is happening, where are your guards?"

Tim was there in a flash, bristling behind me. "What is it?"

"Alpha." The man bowed his head quickly. "A large group is coming. The sentries sense a large amount of mag—□

The messenger was cut off as a wolf song broke through the walls. Sorrowful and haunting, it caused me to shiver, my familiar warning butt tingle making me wrap my magic around me like a cloak. I needed to get the hell out of there. I didn't know how to use my magic well enough, and I didn't have Stefan to protect me. Tim and his crowd were great fighters, but they couldn't balance my potentially fatal draw of magic.

"Get her to safety and then meet me in the front!" Tim pushed past us, moving down the hall with massive, lumbering steps. The bear side of him wasn't far from breaking free.

"Sasha!" I froze at that nightmarish growl.

Jonas stalked up on liquid joints, his tattoos glowing a furious orange. His fierce gaze took in the were-tiger Tim had ordered to escort me to safety. "Run along kitty-cat, I've got her."

A deep growl rumbled out of the man's chest, shaking my bones and making me step to the side, out from between these two wild men. Jonas struck out with his hand, grabbed my arm and dragged me near. The intensity in his eyes shocked into me a second later.

"They're here for you. We gotta get you outta here."

"But... I should fight..." I started, much rather facing a horde of unknowns than this one man alone.

"You fight, you die. The Boss trusted you to my care. You're coming with me."

I stared at the burly man, unsure. He stared back, no expression, turning my bones to liquid. Jonas was right, though, Stefan trusted Jonas for some reason.

I hadn't told Stefan about that first battle. About Jonas leaving me to die in that first battle.

But still, he trusted Jonas, and not the *Mata.* I trusted Stefan. I didn't have much to go off of, so I had to trust the lesser of two evils.

I started to jog next to Jonas, his long, hurried steps nearly impossible for me to keep up with. "Where's Charles?" I asked in as close to a normal voice as I could muster. It sounded like a wobbling, squeaky bicycle.

"Charles can look after himself."

I opened my mouth to push the issue, ducking into the twilight under Jonas's arm. The evening was just falling, creating that strange gloom that hid things even in plain sight. A light breeze ruffled my hair as a surge of magic pounded in my chest. Freezing cold trickled down from the top of my head, a sure sign that those *Dulcha* monsters were near.

"Hurry!" Jonas urged, grabbing me by the arm and yanking.

"Why are we going toward the woods?" I asked, trying to avoid branches that *thwapped* me in the face.

In answer, Jonas turned to me, a vicious glint in his eye. Without uttering a word, he ducked down and scooped me up, immediately starting to jog deep into the trees, the first blast of battle sounding behind us.

Panic welled up, his harsh grip and haste sending pain and uncertainty into my core. I could shock him and get out of his hold, but then what? My power could beat his, but my use of it was truly lacking. Then where would I go? To the front line, where the *Dulcha* would chase and hound me? I couldn't hide. Already I could feel them, seeking me, drawn to my power.

I wiggled, still uncertain, hearing all the warnings over the last few weeks. Everyone had cited Jonas as someone to watch. Someone to steer clear from. Stefan trusted him, yes, but friendship could disillusion a person. And didn't Stefan say he trusted me? That he had faith in me?

But then he'd sent Darla to basically sit on her hands and wait for me to fail.

Tim and the *Mata* were my friends.

I would not fail.

Decided, I sucked power into myself, feeling the darkness as it warred with the daylight, drawing it into myself and feeling my limbs heat. Jonas flinched, trying to hold on, but was unable to as my body electrified to his touch.

He jumped and released me suddenly, leaving me sprawled on the ground.

"What the fuck are you doing?" he asked savagely, reaching down to me with a giant hand. "Do you want to die?"

I scrambled away, ready with a blast of magic. I raised my palm and registered the widening of his eyes just as Adnan burst through the trees ahead of us, his blade glowing red, his throwing star in his hand.

"I knew it, Jonas! Trying to steal away Sasha? You failed last time so you wanted to do it in person this time?"

Darla stepped through the trees next. Sinewy and graceful, she held two deceptively delicate-looking daggers, each glowing deep red. Her confident gaze took in Jonas and she shook her head and tsk'd. "The Boss's childhood friend. But then, we all saw this coming. Didn't we, Adnan?"

"Why are you helping me?" I blurted, focused on Darla.

Her gaze never left Jonas, as she worked with Adnan to block Jonas and myself from continuing on our path.

"I'm not helping *you,* I'm helping the Boss. *You* are just a stupid human. If I save you, I save the day."

"What is it you think you're saving her from?" Jonas growled. "I'm going to the underground safe house to cut off her magic from the *Dulcha.*"

"Would that work?" I asked of no one, which was exactly who paid attention to me.

Chapter 9

Stefan walked through the south-end corridor on the third floor, his focus on the turmoil within the link. With Sasha as far away as she was, he couldn't feel much, but what he did had him disconcerted. She'd been in some state of unhappiness since she left, but this was altogether different.

He saw two flesh covered forms writhing against the wall, one between the legs of the other, thrusting in great swings. Stefan's balls tightened, the three weeks of abstinence playing hell on his concentration.

"Knock it off," Stefan snarled as he passed, stopping the figures in a tight embrace.

The young male looked up with the fervor of lust. He wouldn't dare question orders, but the blank stare said he obviously didn't know why he should refrain.

"There is a ban on sex in this area. We house a pregnant female and her offspring. She does not want her children seeing fornication when they wander out of their rooms."

A red hue suffused the youth's face, the female looking down to hide her embarrassment. They muttered apologies as they disengaged, then hurried away. Shaking his head, Stefan knocked politely, waiting for one of the Shape Changer children to open the door.

Esmine waited inside, lounging on a sofa, rubbing her belly. She looked up at Stefan's entrance, smiling a greeting.

"I came to ensure your continued comfort," Stefan stated, looking over the room to make sure it had been cleaned regularly. He'd stopped by once every few days just to check on her. Seeing all was well, he returned his gaze to the female.

"Yes, thanks," she replied demurely, the lupine gaze he sometimes saw retracted now. "Your people have been kind and gracious."

"You have everything you need?"

"Again, yes, thank you."

A small child bounded over to her, looking at him through the shyness of youth.

"They are enamored with your people," Esmine said with a laugh as she put a comforting hand on the female child's head. "They stare and gawk, only to squeal and giggle when one of the helpers assigned to us plays. I had no idea everyone here was so good with children."

Stefan lounged so as not to appear impatient. "We cherish children here. We try hard for them, and are only rewarded occasionally. We protect them with every fiber of our being."

Esmine nodded. "Continuing the line. We know something of that."

A fast rapping interrupted them, the door swinging open and Jameson marching in. "Boss, we need you."

"What is it?" Esmine asked, rising onto her elbows, her pregnant belly awkward and hindering. "Are we in danger?"

"I assure you, you are not in danger. I will send someone in shortly to fill you in on whatever is happening. We are safe within these walls." Stefan bowed to her. "Excuse me."

"They are planning to attack Sasha's location," Jameson said as soon as they were out of earshot. "For the last three weeks we haven't seen one *Dulcha*. Not one. We've seen increased numbers crossing our borders, but we only engage in skirmishes."

They nearly flew down the stairs, heading to their strategy room where Dominicous would be waiting. "We knew something was up, but couldn't find out what. Then our spy overheard Trek and Andris speaking. They have someone on the inside."

Stefan burst into the strategy room, accounting for each member of their battle council, noting the presence of Rich, Tim's Beta, then taking a seat at the head of the table. Dominicous stood just off to the side, allowing Stefan the authority to preside by removing himself. It was an incredibly helpful gesture of good faith. Not many in the chain of command would relinquish power to one lesser. Stefan understood, however, that it wasn't permanent by any means. Simply expeditious.

"What are their plans?" Stefan asked, focusing on a map in the center of the table.

"They're putting all their efforts into what appears to be Sasha's location. They plan to create one hell of a distraction, killing anyone they can, while a small group spirits Sasha out the back. We should receive a small scale attack here, keeping us busy, and them under the impression they are the only ones with a spy. Andris and Trek will be heading the distraction, though. They do not think they will fail."

"They never think they'll fail. It's their greatest downfall." Stefan considered a minute, the room silent as he weighed the options. "Send a team in right now. We may be too late, but we need to at least warn the Shape Changers. We'll leave a group here to defend the mansion, but we need to gear up and meet Trek head on."

"Another team, you mean?" Andrew asked, his face screwed up in puzzlement.

"What do you mean *another* team?" Stefan shot back as Dominicous straightened.

Andrew shook his head in jerky movements. "Maybe I'm wrong, but Adnan, a student of mine, mentioned he wouldn't be around because he was personally asked to help warn Sasha of a spy. He said it was a test of his skills so that he might make the Watch Command. He went with Darla and someone else. I thought him a little young for the assignment, but he has great rapport with Sasha, so I didn't question your judgment—else I would have asked you about it."

"Darla?" Stefan asked in controlled fury. "When did they leave?" And how the hell had Darla known Sasha's location when even he had not been told?

"About two weeks ago, if I'm not mistaken."

"I haven't seen Darla around," another council member added thoughtfully.

Fear froze Stefan's insides. "We haven't any time to lose. Get Esmine and the children to a safe location. Rally everyone else."

*****

The ground shook with an explosion, the telltale sign I'd be caught up in yet another battle. What had happened to my quiet life of boredom and *hoping* for some action? I missed those days.

"C'mon, Sasha, come over here," Adnan said, his sword pointing at Jonas's face.

"You two are under the impression you can take me, is that it? Did anyone happen to mention she shoots black?" Jonas asked in his scary voice.

"I wasn't planning to deal with you myself." Darla laughed.

"You were planning to let a child handle me, then?" Jonas stepped forward slowly, experienced and lethal. Adnan was good for his age, but Jonas had many years on him with the added bonus of unparalleled viciousness.

"Not at all. I brought the child to appear legit. He was too stupid to realize what was going on, unlike my other lackey. She had to be put down."

She must have been talking about Mira! Sasha felt a rush of fury at the cruel injustice.

Darla looked over her shoulder at six men at arms stepping through the foliage.

"Shit," Jonas swore, taking another step, this time in front of me.

"You see, I come prepared," Darla continued. "Thanks for getting her this far, though. Underground was a great idea, but short lived."

Adnan blinked, his sword lowering, his attention bouncing back and forth between Darla, the new additions—which apparently didn't belong to Stefan's clan—and Jonas. I was doing the same thing. Darla had always been a bitch, but never a double-crossing bitch. Jonas, on the other hand, had never struck me as trustworthy.

As if hearing my thoughts, and desperate to disband them, Jonas shouted, "Sasha, *run*!" He launched his body forward, bypassing Adnan and aiming directly for the first man through the trees.

"Grab her!" Darla shouted, propelling toward me.

Adnan, finally catching on, stepped in front of her, his blade whirling.

That's all I saw. Afraid to do magic lest I accidentally blow up the good guys, I ran. No destination in mind, just *away.* I would not be captured again. Trek and Andris knew what I was now. I was sure of it. If they were coming for me again, they didn't plan to let me go once they got me.

A blind panicked run later I heard the first screech of an animal in pain. That sorrowful dog's wail, so much worse, somehow, than a human screaming or crying. The wail cut off abruptly.

My every instinct urged me to find a place to hide and wait all this out. But if I did that, I would forever be a coward. No matter if I made up for it later by somehow winning the whole war single-handedly, I would always remember that first battle where I skulked away and let other people die on my behalf.

The caped moron and his minions had come to this place because of me. Andris fought these people to acquire me as a prize. People were dying and screaming on my behalf.

To save me. In what world could I live with that knowledge, without helping them fight back?

No world I wanted to live in, that was for sure.

"Damn it!" I sprinted toward my cabin, darted through the door and pawed through my possessions. One thing was for certain, I had to have my trusty rape whistle. It had always been good luck in these sorts of things, and by God, it would see me through. Obviously I grabbed my dagger, too. I wasn't a complete idiot.

With that, I sprinted back out, my chest throbbing with the magic in the air, proof the *Dulcha* were in the area. I might as well just call the damn things. They'd seek me out anyway.

At a jog I aimed for the heart of the most noise, the night flickering bright with explosions or blasts of spells. Looming trees illuminated with a rainbow of glows for seconds at a time, serious spells and charms zinging around the place. Apparently the caped white mage had found the non-caped variety. I had no doubt Toa was winning.

Until I got closer.

Dodging in between the trees with the agility born of someone I wasn't, I saw a blast of white leave the fingers of a glowing blond ghost, his hair flying in the breeze like feathers, so like the vampires in the stories, with his graceful elegance and ethereal beauty, I nearly recoiled thinking another magical kind of person had shown up. As a huge wolf bounded in front of me, teeth bared in a drool-flinging snarl, I properly saw what Toa was up against. How *many* Toa was up against.

Trek stood some distance away on a rock outcropping, blasting spell after attack spell Toa's way. Those, Toa seemed to block without too much concern, wiping them aside with a defensive spell, and then throwing his own in return. The problem was the *Dulcha.* There were dozens aiming for Toa, giant beasts with fangs and claws, hurling magic or flailing razor-sharp claws. Some even created other representations of themselves, spinning charms and spells as if they were human.

A sickening realization hit me. They *were* human—at least the essence of them. The body long since dead, their blood and Trek's magic had created these disgusting monsters. Toa didn't have any *Dulcha* because he wasn't a murderer of innocent people. The very thought of it was as revolting as it was rage inspiring.

Toa had to cast three spells to Trek's one. Stefan had sent less than half a dozen warriors. The *Mata*, for their part, fought fiercely, tooth and claw biting and scratching beast or man, able to cut through monsters like magically coated blades. So, we had some brawn, but not a lot of magic throwers.

No pressure.

Here we go, let's add some of my own monsters to the mix!

I pulled up the sleeves of my hoodie and let the magic fill me. Calling the elements, I drew in so much fire my face felt hot.

Three wolves surrounded me, facing out, snarling and growling as one. Now two

Dulcha noticed me on the scene. That, of course, drew enemy eyes. One even pointed.

Howdy boys and girls! Wanna see a magic show?

I sent a blast of orange toward a tree way behind enemy lines, my power going up in an arc and falling like a star. I always made the absolute best monsters with orange. In the dark distance I could see a tree burst into magical fire, orange flame licking up the side into the top, the whole thing shimmering until a huge foot yanked out of the ground.

I sent another. They would come toward me, trampling and killing anything in their path. That would get Trek looking.

I tried to take off toward Toa, but a snarling wolf cut me off, the three—now four guard wolves—trying to herd me out of harm's way.

"Do you want to die? Because without me you have no chance unless you run!" I raised my voice high, trying to throw it over the sounds of howling from my tree creations.

"Move!" I yelled.

The wolf in front of me stuck its tail between its legs, whining as I ran around it. A second later they tailed me, watching my back and flanks like a hunting party.

I shot past a vicious tiger, a massive paw slashing through the chest of his opponent. Blood and guts spilled out to the ground, making me gag.

Near Toa, I saw a giant—and I mean *giant*—Kodiak bear, wielding huge claws with the sharp intellect of Tim. He stood over fifteen feet tall when upright, swiping at *Dulcha* with hundreds of pounds of raw power. Bodies were ripped in half if they got too close, monsters with twisted heads and strange bodies came apart like statues made of leather, then puffed into smoke. Still, he could barely keep them at bay, those attacking making clones of themselves somehow, shooting magic and drifting toward Toa.

Time to sound the siren.

"Leave the *Dulcha* to me!" I screamed.

The shaggy bear's head swung toward me, huge tufted ears twitching. He stood on his back legs, his massive body dwarfing all those around him, while he let out a ground-shaking roar.

I sucked in the magic, feeling my chest spark, a flame within, glowing to life. Hotter and hotter the magic around me swirled, my limbs catching on fire, my skin prickling. More and more, calling those monsters, one or three at a time, tempting them with my raw power.

"Here monster, monster, monster. *Join me!"*

Huge men came at me, glowing tattoos and swords, trying to cut me down where I stood. They felt my draw, felt me calling the power, like the North Pole attracts compass needles. Wolves surged forward, keeping the enemy at bay, letting me call the monsters.

The tiger jumped in my path, launching at a six and a half foot guy about to strike at me, the tiger's jaw fitting around the guy's head. I turned my head away as the head popped off.

I held the power, the magic pulsing out in waves, turning every *Dulcha* in my direction. I saw my tree men, wanting a piece of that action, too. This was about to get messy.

I blasted some trees while I waited, red streams firing out from my hands. I sent a spiral of flame toward Trek, a satisfied laugh filling me as his cap caught on fire. My laugh turned into giddy cackling, the magic infusing my body and prickling my skin.

I needed to release soon. I couldn't totally shut off the tide.

"Clear out of the way," I instructed my growing mass of animal body guards as the first five heinous monsters glided my way.

Blue or purple, they weren't packing much; more like Halloween glow lights than actual threats.

"*Join me!*" they called in their eerie speech of what sounded like consonants. "*I promise great rewards…*"

I pushed out my open palm like a stop motion, and then curled it around and up, grabbing the air around them. I squeezed with my fist, the magic acting out my miming, bending their bodies and exploding the magic out of them.

Sweat beaded my brow, more energy taken than I had anticipated. Not good.

I threw out two red jets, blasting open a tree and scattering whatever attack pattern the enemy had tried for. A red jet came my way, trying to bind me.

"I know how to break that one, now." My black magic crept into the fibers and disintegrated the spell.

I threw out another tree monster, one of the first two having been taken down. I erupted some hives of blue beetles way far away from me, the pests climbing on anything in their path and magically biting legs and faces and whatever they could get at. It wouldn't kill anyone, but it sure hurt like bloody hell.

White exploded around me, knocking me off my feet. I landed in a bush ten feet away, my ears ringing, my leg screaming, surrounded by *Dulcha.* I sat up groggily, furry bodies leaping to my aid, standing in front of me, fangs showing and hair bristling. A panther jumped down from a tree branch onto the nearest monster, scratching and clawing the thing to bits.

My leg pounded along with my heartbeat. One attempt to get up had my shin bursting with agony and my head swimming. I leaned against the bush and shielded myself from future Trek attacks. It would drain me every time his magic hit my shield, but that was the good thing about having more power than him, he'd drain faster than me. Eat *that*!

I zapped off a few fraying spells, my magic wrapping around three *Dulcha,* unraveling the fabric of their spells. It seemed to work okay, the creatures disintegrating like a sugar witch in the rain. I zipped off a couple more as white exploded against my shield.

That asshole is starting to piss me off! Just to be a bitch, I fired off a spell in his direction, a zap of pure electricity. He blocked it, the fiend, but it sucked more energy out of him than he was probably used to.

Back to the never ending monsters. I needed to learn more aggressive spells.

I created a tree monster too close. Crap! I fired fraying spells at will, my aim not great under pressure, but the mass of magical bodies starting to crowd around me making even a misfire useful. Smoky wisps clouded my vision, and still they came. Trek must have brought his whole damn arsenal. He was trying for genocide.

"I need you to move me," I shouted to four furry bodies slashing at monsters in front of me. "I can't walk on my leg, but we need distance. They'll follow me wherever I go; I just have to get there. Somewhere."

Before the first wolf could get in position, the tiger jogged closer, his movements elegant and graceful even though his back was as high as my chest.

He gave one growl and a head jerk.

Get on.

"You are huge, and I think my leg is broken," I responded, zipping out a few more spells, needing the wolves to start ripping and tearing with vigor as the masses drew closer. It was like a mosh pit at a rock concert.

A mountain lion padded up, his baby-like cry having my bones vibrating. I'd heard real mountain lions when they came down from the mountains, and their screech terrified me.

At least, I'd thought it was a real mountain lion at the time…

The tiger growled and jerked its head again, the smaller lion—though not by any means small—acting like a step ladder to boost me up. The wolves' snarls drowned out the night, the monsters starting to wade closer.

I grabbed fur and fell toward the mountain lion, half doing a pull-up, half hopping, to get my good leg on its back. I clawed myself higher, the radiating pain in my shin wanting to blot out my consciousness with each pulse of pure agony.

Eye on the prize, I threw my body over the tiger's back, and then swung my bad leg over his haunches, screaming with the pain. Taking big steadying breaths, I blasted a black spell in Trek's direction, the magic silky, like an oil slick on water, as it wound through the air--then splashed off his defenses. I'd made that one special, though. It would act like acid, slowly eating away power levels as it burrowed in. It would deplete me, also, but I needed the end in sight. With my leg like it was, I didn't have long before the pain and shock took me under. I was already starting to get cold, and it had only been a few minutes. My body had started to shut down.

Okay, time to get serious.

Clutching onto the tiger's back, not knowing his intention and deciding I didn't care—I didn't plan to get off—I thought back to the first time I used a spell on the *Dulcha.* Somehow I had blasted into the fiber of the thing and reached the root to its magic, going back to the source and cutting off the flow of power. Somehow.

Pain making my head throb, I closed my eyes, not worrying about tears. I felt those bastards floating closer, drifting toward my magic like sharks to blood. I also felt my magical acid dripping into Trek's defenses, his power eroding and him not knowing why.

My cheek lay on surprisingly soft tiger fur. I didn't even stick out my palm. I envisioned a beating heart at the center of each monster, a cord from its body to the source of magic. I created magical shears, so black that light penetrated, bent to it, and got lost in its gaping maw. I plunged those shears into the first beast, rooting around, finding what felt like a well of palpitating magic, and *snipped.*

Magic was sucked out of me. The spell was trying to reach every *Dulcha*, of which there were hundreds. The magic drew from my body and looked for more when I started to run out. I opened myself up wide, drawing it out of the air, stealing it from Trek's shield, borrowing it from the tiger and surrounding wolves, and calling to Stefan through the link, begging him for help.

Toa's voice echoed through my head. "Once the spell has been created, it will need to run its course. Your magic is different than mine. With your magic, there is no turning off the faucet once you have set it in motion. You will ride it until it completes the spell, or it drains enough energy to kill you."

"So that's what he meant," I said weakly, my head getting fuzzy. "There are so many," I mumbled as the magic drained faster than I could fill.

Then I felt a surge. A great swell of swirling elements up through my middle, refilling me with energy as I lay on the tiger's back, fading. Stefan was replenishing me. He was close! How had I missed that?

I felt more than saw a burnished gold sword held by flashing tattoos on rippled arms, the blade fading to gold as my eyes drooped, his power diminishing with what he was giving me. I could potentially kill both of us unless he cut off his donation. Which he wouldn't. But there was nothing I could do.

Protect the tiger! I heard through the haze.

As blackness consumed me, my body shutting down from the magical trauma and agony from my leg, I heard a bloodcurdling scream wrench the night. My spell had indirectly reached the source, cutting off the last *Dulcha* from Trek's original spell. It probably hurt worse than my leg. Like ripping out a kidney without drugs.

"Capture him!" someone yelled.

My mind stopped comprehending. I felt empty. The battle raged, part of the enemy faction trying to get to me, but others running in another direction.

I began to hear their screams and calls to retreat. And then I felt my last remaining tree monster. I didn't have the energy to cut the power.

"Get moving. Take her to safety." Stefan's voice sounded like angels singing.

I reached my hand out, trying to touch him, only seeing a hazy orange glow.

"Charles, with Sasha. Take the wolves. I'll help Tim," Stefan ordered.

I had a lot to live up to if I hoped to match his prowess for command. He wasn't even directing his own people and they rushed to follow his lead.

I let my mind get even hazier as we moved away from the yelling and sword clashes. Stefan had probably brought his people, which meant the fight was nearly done. Sleep would happen soon. Or fever. We'd see.

Chapter 10

"How is she?" the Boss demanded as he entered the *Mata* hospital cabin twenty-four hours after the battle.

Charles got up immediately from his chair by Sasha's head and moved to the other side of the bed. "She's okay. Compound fracture in her leg, so that's going to take ages to heal. She's a human, after all. Toa helped a little with a spell, but he didn't say how much that would speed it up. Bumps and bruises, she'll probably be extremely weak with magic for a few days, but other than that she'll survive."

The Boss lowered himself into the chair, gently taking up Sasha's hand where it rested on the bed. Charles had never seen the man move so delicately, careful not to disturb her. Seeing this form of vulnerability made him nervous; he knew that on the other side of it was a white hot rage that would destroy anything in its path. Charles stepped away toward the window.

Technically, it wasn't Charles's fault she'd ended up like this. Jonas had gotten to her first and tried to move her to safety. Out of everyone, no one had thought Darla was smart enough to get in league with Andris and his goons. No one had suspected her of anything more than trying to drown Sasha and steal the Boss back. This was a stretch, even for her. Which was probably why it had worked out badly.

Still, Jonas had barely gotten away with his life. If not for Adnan, he probably wouldn't have survived. If Charles had been in his place, he had to admit that things might've worked out differently. Charles should have been involved; should have found Sasha and taken her to safety. She'd nearly died. If not for the Boss, she would have. All to save everyone else. Which was ass backward as far as the plan had gone.

"What were the losses?" Charles asked, throwing his gaze out the window so he could stop registering the tender look on the Boss's face. That shit made him uncomfortable.

"The *Mata* lost a dozen or so, mostly in the first scuffle. Another dozen are wounded and chained to the bed for a while. The *Dulcha* wreaked havoc. Trek must have emptied his store of captives to create that many. They know, without a doubt, what Sasha could represent, and they want her. Or, they want to destroy her."

"What of Trek, and Andris? Could you get them?"

A smug look crossed the Boss's face. "I got Trek. Sasha knocked the breath out of him and I got there in time to take out his guard and scoop him up. Dominicous and Toa are seeing to him. They plan to take him back to the Council."

"Andris?" Charles was half afraid to ask. Andris was the brains behind the operation, working with whomever necessary to internationally to make their uprising a household name. His level of ambition bordered on an obsession, and his intelligence made everything possible.

The Boss shook his head. "Once he realized the tide was turning, he got skittish. I saw him briefly as I grabbed Trek, but he was already on his way out."

"So, what does that mean for the Eastern Territory?"

Stefan brushed some wisps of hair back from Sasha's bruised and scratched face. Charles turned away again. "We won't have any problems for a while—Andris will probably join up with another faction to regroup. He'll search for another way to accomplish his goals. We'll have a reprieve from fighting for a while."

"Quiet before the storm."

The Boss nodded slowly.

Andris was a tricky bastard; the only thing you could count on with him was unpredictability. It made strategy a nightmare.

Or so the Boss said.

*****

I opened my eyes and surveyed my room, greeted by the same spotless white affair with that chemical smell you seem to only find in hospitals. While I wasn't in an actual hospital, I had been moved to a room in the encampment that acted like one.

I turned my head to the side, expecting, and finding, my new B.F.F. lying in the bed beside mine, healing. It had been three days since the battle, and two days since Jonas was moved into my room. Apparently, he didn't want to be removed from my side, even in the hospital. Somehow, when he'd sacrificed himself to prevent me from being taken, his mind had made the connection that I was worth saving. Charles had said once that thought entered Jonas's head that was it. Cemented.

"Quit staring, human."

Being that there was no TV, and he hated reading, Jonas had nothing better to do than to talk to me. Instead, he stared straight at the ceiling. He still hadn't forgiven me for being human.

I had now forgiven him for leaving me that first battle.

"Did you eat recently?" I asked. I could usually get a response with simple questions that had some relevance.

"Why?"

"I'm hungry."

"How is that my problem?"

"It isn't. You'll notice I didn't accuse you of eating. I merely asked if you did, wondering if I missed a meal during my beauty sleep."

Jonas huffed. "Better get back to sleep. You still look like dog shit."

"Uh hum. So…did you eat?"

His bruised and battered face scrunched down into a tight ball, his desire to ignore me fighting with his need to keep me alive. He hated me even more for it. It caused me no end of chuckling. Especially now that I knew he wouldn't kill me.

"No. Lunch is coming in about half an hour." Jonas resumed staring at the ceiling.

He'd sustained a plethora of broken bones, got pounded on, had magical burns and other strange magical maladies, but he'd killed all the enemy invaders with the help of Adnan. Darla had gotten away, had run as soon as I was out of reach, but no one seemed overly concerned with that fact. Other than me, obviously. She was a crazy bitch, not to mention a scorned woman

The door opened slowly. Charles peeked in, scanned the room's occupants, grinned at Jonas, and then winked at me. "You want a visitor?"

"How the hell can we get any peace and quiet with the human getting damn visitors all day?" Jonas growled at Charles.

Charles's grin widened. "Bro, you need to simmer down. People are going to think you aren't friendly."

"I'll show you friendly," Jonas muttered, looking back at the ceiling. It was the only place to direct his eyes away from people. The nurse had tried to lean over him to maintain eye contact when it was time to change his bandages. That nurse had left with a black eye. Apparently hitting Shape Changer females wasn't the same as human females. Which made sense—the ladies were nearly as strong as the guys, and just as great at fighting.

The nurse had leaned on Jonas's broken ribs in retaliation.

Tim entered the room with his strangely graceful lumber, the way he walked characteristic of the ginormous Kodiak bear he turned into. He sauntered to the chair at the head of my bed, picked it up and moved to the other side so his face was to Jonas. Not many *Mata* trusted Jonas, even though he'd done the right thing by me.

"Sasha," Tim said as his soft brown eyes met mine. "How are you feeling?"

I shrugged. "Okay. The pain meds make me feel better. My shin stopped throbbing, too, so I think I'm good for the moment."

"I'd thought you were safe; that you had been taken to safety. I apologize. You should not have been in that battle."

"I could've been safe—I think—but I couldn't let your people die for me."

Jonas huffed, drawing Tim's alpha st for a moment. Jonas ignored him.

Tim refocused on me, his face softening instantly. "We were grossly outnumbered. You saved a great many lives. I, and the pack, would like to thank you. You have our favor, and are anointed Pack Friend status. Should you need us, for any reason, we will be there for you. As kin."

"Wow." I blinked for a moment, taken aback. "But I stepped on someone in order to ride your tiger like a horse. Surely a few people are a little…miffed."

Tim's lips quirked. "Like I said, you saved a great many lives. You showed bravery and courage, even with a bone poking out of your leg. The tiger didn't mind a beautiful woman riding him."

"Be careful with your flirting," Jonas warned, his eyes boring holes in the ceiling tiles. "She is marked."

"Marked?" Tim asked, his eyes scanning all available skin.

"By the Boss, I elaborated. "Humans can't smell it. Or sense it, or whatever. It's a chemical thing." "Well, then, I guess it doesn't apply outside of Stefan's kind," Tim smiled this time, a predatory gleam in his eyes, mocking Jonas. I rolled my eyes.

"What about Ann? Is she okay?" I held my breath.

Tim smiled. "Just fine. A few scratches is all."

I let my breath out. I'd only talked to her a few times, but I liked her, and I badly needed a friend that was a girl.

"Anyway," Tim said, his warm hand clasping mine. "I'll check back in with you later. Let me know if you want me to find you a room a little less…occupied."

"Yes, do find her a room less occupied," Jonas piped up immediately. "Her incessant talking does my head in."

"Sweet, ain't he?" I asked with a grin.

*****

I stood in front of a congregation of Stefan's clan, wearing a sheer black gown, denoting my magic level. Stefan stood next to me, wearing a sheer suit in burnished gold. In front of him stood Dominicous, Toa by his side, both showing off their magical levels. Also sheer.

I had never seen so many people basically naked in all my life. Unfortunately, I couldn't be stressed out by that fact. It was unfortunate because what did have me stressed out was a lot more important.

"I stand before you, as your Regional, to proclaim Sasha your mage. Linked with your leader, Stefan, with at least two Watch Commanders sworn to throw down their lives to protect her, Charles and Jonas, she fulfills the requirements for this post. Take notice."

Everyone in the room, whether they liked me or not, bowed their heads. I saw more than one hostile stare as faces turned back up—more than one person that wanted to fit me for cement shoes and take me to the lake—but they could not deny my power level. They had no one else for the role.

"Sasha comes to us with the highest power level ever recorded," Dominicous continued, his voice rising above those gathered. "She has thrice battled our mortal enemy, and come out on top. Take notice."

Again with the near naked bowing; something slightly gross and weird, both at the same time.

"In addition, she has tied herself with the *Mata*, a lost connection we hoped to re-forge. A connection already shown to yield positive results. Through her, they are tied with us. Take notice."

Stefan gave the barest of flinches, his hands balling for a fraction of a second. He controlled himself easily, his eyes still trained on Dominicous.

"Welcome her within our fold. We expect great things from her." Dominicous winked at me, intending for me to bow. Which I did, trying my hardest not to cover my lady bits in mortification.

The gathered crowd bowed back. And that was that. I now had a job I was only qualified for when in the middle of a war, battle, or any life and death situation. It could be worse, I guess. I could've been kicked out of the territory. At least I still had a home.

After Dominicous nodded, and Toa nodded, and Stefan nodded—too many chiefs—the congregation broke up. Dominicous stepped up to me immediately, offering me his arm. Stefan stepped back, and then turned to see to other matters while Dominicous led me toward a banquet in my honor.

"You did exceedingly well, Sasha," he said quietly. "I am exceptionally proud of you.

He hesitated, stopping in an isolated corner. "Stefan told you of how we first met?"

Shivers raked my body.

"Do you remember?" he asked, his sharp gaze focused on me.

I shook my head. "But I've always been able to see your kind. My foster parents thought something was wrong with me until I stopped mentioning it."

Dominicous titled his head thoughtfully. "It is an interesting topic. One I might like to explore. If we expose human children to us, maybe even share our blood, will they grow to be able to access their magical gifts? It bears thinking about."

I guess. "What parents are going to give you access to their kids?"

"Kids without parents need a proper home. You were lucky to find one. Many don't. I wonder if I can do good, while also conducting a large scale experiment. It bears thinking about."

Obviously, he would think about it. I just nodded distractedly. I wasn't in the mood to think. I was in the mood to cover up, lie down, and share a quiet evening alone with Stefan.

And yet here I was, the guest of honor at a party while wearing a see-through gown. Sweet Jesus, how did I get myself into these things?

Seeing my discomfort, Dominicous smiled. "We'll speak more thoroughly at a later date. I can see now is not the time." He directed me toward my prince, standing at the head of the room in unshakable confidence, just as naked as me, but caring not at all. My heart surged and my body filled with warmth. His gaze swiveled to me immediately.

"I approve of your choice, by the way," Dominicous said as we slowly walked closer, my hand lightly holding his arm. "He is young for his post, but more than deserving. You have found a worthy mate."

My face heated and my body shivered, responding to the implications of that word. "I love him."

"Yes. And he you. It is a good match. We'll make sure it's a lasting one."

I smiled at Dominicous in thanks as he handed me off to Stefan.

"How are you now, love?" Stefan asked quietly. Charles had made himself scarce.

"I need a robe." I pointed my chest at Stefan so no one could see my boobies. Not that they were looking. There were a lot bigger ones on display.

"You did well in that battle, though we'll talk about why you were there."

I gulped. Stefan had been taking it easy on me for the last couple months since I'd largely been an invalid, but I knew it wouldn't last forever, especially now that my leg was nearly back to new. He hated seeing me in danger. Regardless if it was now my post to take on bad guys, he still didn't like it. If it was up to him, I'd be stashed away in a tamperproof box during all dangerous situations.

"When can we leave?"

Stefan wrapped his arm around my back. "You need to stay for a while longer. You need to be seen with your new clan. You're one of us, now. You're a viable member. You're mine."

My body tingled. Yes, I was. One hundred percent his. I always had been. And now I had a home. These people didn't completely accept me yet, but now I had proven I had a right to be here. Gaining their trust was in my hands. I was on the doorstep to finally belonging somewhere. The prospects had me giddy.

Though, the nudity would take some getting used to.

I took a deep breath and smiled. It had been a long road, but finally, I didn't have any secrets. I could just be me.

*****

Dominicous turned to Toa as Sasha entwined hands with Stefan. "Did you speak to her about her ability to communicate with the *Dulcha*? Does she realize what that means?"

Toa studied the remarkable young woman with a great many secrets, many she had yet to learn. "I did not. There is no reason to worry her just yet. That is a skill we will have to harness, however. It won't be long before we see a more powerful demon not relegated to the confines of a human body, as the *Dulcha* are."

"And you think her ability it is a result of that crash?"

"I think so. I can find no other explanation."

Dominicous shifted, his gaze settling back on Sasha. "I wonder why she survived, when no one else did. It wasn't magic—not in one so young. She saw us before I gave her blood, too. Remember that? Stared us down defiantly after she tumbled out of the ripped carnage. After she stumbled our way. Almost as if she walked away from that accident and specifically toward us. Crossing the human divide at that time, rather than when she met

Stefan. Was it luck, or does Fate still have her in its grip?"

Toa blinked. "If Fate, what does it want with her? And how does Stefan play into it…?"

"How do we?"

"You will need to link with her," Dominicous said after a while. "As a white power level, it will give her much needed protection. Whatever Fate's plans, she needs to be armed with as much as we can give her."

"But how to convince her? She is a strong-willed woman—not one to easily manipulate. She will not want to go against Stefan's wishes, and his primal urge to possess her will cloud his judgment. He will not want any other male to have a hold on her, even if it is to help."

Dominicous gave a smug smile. "She has attracted a strong and sure suitor. I could not have picked better. I've chosen well for my protégés. When I rise, I will yank Stefan and her up behind me. If we confront the murmurings of treason within the Council, we will do it with a strong backing of power."

"Yes. Though I still hope those whispered fears are unfounded..."

Dominicous kept silent. He did not know, but they'd need to figure it out soon. Danger was mounting.

THE END

Printed in Great Britain
by Amazon